2017-486

S0-BAW-727

WOHTVALE PUBLIC LIBRARY

INSIDE

INSIDE V

PAULA PRIAMOS

THIS IS A GENUINE VIREO BOOK

A Vireo Book | Rare Bird Books
453 South Spring Street, Suite 302
Los Angeles, CA 90013
rarebirdbooks.com

Copyright © 2017 by Paula Priamos

FIRST TRADE PAPERBACK ORIGINAL EDITION

All rights reserved, including the right to reproduce this book or portions
thereof in any form whatsoever, including but not limited to print, audio, and
electronic. For more information, address: A Vireo Book | Rare Bird Books
Subsidiary Rights Department, 453 South Spring Street, Suite 302,
Los Angeles, CA 90013.

Set in Dante
Printed in the United States

10 9 8 7 6 5 4 3 2 1

Publisher's Cataloging-in-Publication data.
Names: Priamos, Paula, author.
Title: Inside V / Paula Priamos.
Description: First Trade Paperback Original Edition | A Genuine Vireo Book |
New York, NY; Los Angeles, CA: Rare Bird Books, 2017.
Identifiers: ISBN 9781945572074
Subjects: LCSH Marriage—Fiction. | Adultery—Fiction. | Betrayal—Fiction.
| Sex offenders—Fiction. | Suspense fiction. | Mystery and detective stories. |
BISAC FICTION / Mystery & Detective / General
Classification: LCC PS3616 .R496 I5 2017 | DDC 813.6—dc23

MONTVALE PUBLIC LIBRARY

CHAPTER ONE

COLOR SCHEME

Such a tranquil shade is risky. To some on the jury, any range of blue might appear too cool, too emotionally removed. A tie, a simple strip of fabric, should never carry so much weight. As a former public defender, I know this and maybe a part of me wants jurors to know this, too. The rest of what my husband will be wearing today—a white button down shirt and a charcoal gray suit—lie out on our bed like missing parts of a man I used to know.

Beside the blue tie there is the brick red one to consider. Red is a red flag no matter which hue—he is too Republican, too much of the stereotype of a white rich guy. As an investment banker it would mean two strikes against him even though it's his clients' money he invests, hardly ever his own. And Grant and I are both registered Independents.

Or more obviously, red reminds people of lust which is the last feeling my husband, given his circumstances, should be reminding anyone of.

I hear him in the shower washing off, *washing her off,* a seventeen-year-old Latina girl he is accused of sexually assaulting. There is no getting rid of her, not with soap or a sandblaster. My husband is on trial in a Los Angeles courtroom for statutory rape. The trial has been fast tracked in less than seven months because Grant is anxious to clear his name. He wants us to reclaim the marriage we once had before I got the call the night of his arrest.

The time had been 8:13 p.m.

On the hardwood floor in the family room, I paced heavily and loudly in sky-high wedges as if I'd just been weighted down by bricks. I asked the stranger on the other end of the line, a female staff member of my husband's newly hired legal team, to repeat the charges. Every time she tried to get out the words, I kept interrupting, because although I'd asked I really couldn't bear to hear them again, the unspeakable sex charges, all felonies. "You're sure this isn't some kind of mistake? I mean he...he wouldn't *do this.*" Irrationally I wished I was right, that she'd called the wrong house and my husband would walk through the front door, a little East Coast rushed like the native he is, his suit barely wrinkled and his tie torn loose around his neck, half assembled, the way he moves around all morning before he leaves for work. He'd give me a slow kiss before jokingly informing me he had the car still running as if *I* was the one who'd made us late for our Friday night dinner reservation. We'd laugh about the call on the ride to the restaurant how one unlucky son of a bitch had a lot of explaining to do with his wife.

The irony was not lost on me. I was wearing skinny jeans, a sweater, and the wedges. While Grant was allegedly forcing the clothes off a seventeen-year-old girl, I was here at home dressing up for him, putting on his favorite outfit. Our usual Friday date night had turned into a nightmare I have yet to wake up from. Someone had decided that the news of Grant's arrest would be easier coming from another woman instead of my own husband. Only a coward would deny his wife the right to hang up on him.

Grant and I had had dinner reservations for eight thirty at Westley's, a pricey new steakhouse located down the street atop the second story of a strip mall. The place touted sawdust on the floors, mason jars for glasses, and imitation log walls.

"Seriously?" I'd said when my husband had suggested we eat there. "Westley's?"

"Yeah," Grant laughed in that hearty, chest-deep way that sounded fake, only it wasn't. "What's the matter with Westley's?"

I shrugged.

"The name makes me think of some pale-faced pervert coming out of a sex shop with his pants down." My own punch line is no longer so funny now that my husband is accused of something far worse than indecent exposure. I wonder if Grant stands under that beating hard water and regrets letting the girl take a seat across from him in the booth at Monty's Restaurant and Bar on Wilshire Boulevard that late afternoon. Over and over again, he's told me that nothing more than a drink passed between them, and I want to believe him. Sometimes I even convince myself that I do.

"I love you, V," he says. V is the nickname he's come up with for me instead of calling me by my first name, Ava. He touches my face gently, though his jaw is clenched, upset that his words aren't getting through to me. "I would never cheat on you. It's you I see when I close my eyes when we're fucking. *You are my fantasy.*"

Before the trial, before all those months leading up to it, before the phone call that informed me of the charges, Grant and I were all over each other inside this house. We weren't that married couple who made love only on weekends on the matrimonial bed. We were a married couple who loved each other but also still fucked each other at random hours of the day. Grant might catch me off guard in the kitchen waiting for coffee to brew or playfully feel up my tank while I was trying to scramble eggs.

Sometimes we wound up both calling in late for work in order to properly finish what he'd started. Neither one of us ever left the bed without the other climaxing. We never parted between our cars warming in the driveway without kissing, without saying we loved one another.

Now our physical contact is reduced to public handholding that starts from the outside of the car in the parking structure of the courthouse through the ride up the elevator to the third floor, in case a juror happens to spot us. Grant doesn't push for more. He understands he's asked too much of me already. And now I've been asked by his lawyer, Reynolds Wilson, an overpaid shyster with two last names, to select Grant's outfit today of all days when the Latina Girl is the next witness to testify for the prosecution. My husband's victim if you are to believe the charges. If he's found guilty he could serve a year in prison and be required to register as a sex offender for the rest of his life.

The betrayal feels nothing short of a dizzying blow to the back of the head because I never saw it coming. Everyone assumes I am the injured, devastated wife. But it is only the role I'm playing for the jury. Some might say, like mother like daughter, that I am only waiting for the right time to violently get even with my husband. They would be wrong, of course. I'm nothing like the hot-blooded, homicidal Greek woman who knew no other means but a bullet in his back to stop my father from walking out on her. I was twelve when I watched it happen. She used his own gun. My father was a cop, but now he's in a wheelchair.

I hear the shower water turn off as I head back to my husband's dresser drawer where the rest of his ties are laid out in neat rows like a table display you'd find in a department store. Grant is a man of meticulous order, which is why this mess of things he's made with the Latina Girl is unlike him. It *isn't* him, not even with the prosecutor continuously throwing hard liquor in the mix.

In exchange for the blue and red ties I select a paisley one Grant never wears, a gift from my father or his. Such a hideous pattern might distract the jurors from the ugly truth that a man as handsome as my husband is accustomed to getting away with anything.

CHAPTER TWO

PARTIAL TESTIMONY OF THE LATINA GIRL

The first thing I notice about my husband's accuser is that she has nubs, not in reference to her breasts, but the tips of her nails. They're bitten down to the pinks. I pass by her in the hall on my way into the courtroom. She will wait out here until court starts and she is called to the stand to testify. All I can think about are the missing whites of her nails, the physical sign of a worrier or worse, a victim. My fear is those chewed down nails will prove more effective than her broken English with the jury should she turn distraught and cover her face with her hands.

The most remarkable thing about her is that her face looks nothing like mine. Call it selfish relief, but it's relief none the same to know my husband wasn't seeking a similar yet ethnically different, younger copy of me. Her hair is a dark sheet and her eyes are dangerously downcast. The jury will be more prone to want to lock eyes with her, connect with whatever emotion she's feeling on the stand. She's wearing a thin flowery sundress that isn't right for this time of year, even in Southern California. But the outfit makes her look more innocent. The Latina Girl has recently turned eighteen. Possibly a deliberate move by the prosecutor, an old dog named Henry Daniels who knows all the tricks, even going so far as to use his advanced age in the courtroom by purposely stooping over, when in reality he has the rail-rod spinal cord of a man half his age.

A fat man, dark skinned and bald, practically takes up the entire front row, the Latina Girl's father. His arm rests across a good portion of the empty space of the bench, and he keeps checking his watch as though he's saving the spot for someone. If it's emotional support the Latina Girl is after, she might have to look elsewhere. There is something about him that strikes me as hard, the kind of stern father who would rather ready his belt to punish his kids because he has no patience for time outs or reprimands. The Latina Girl has an eleven or twelve-year-old brother who is not in the courtroom, neither apparently is their mother. I've seen her name on the witness list. In case the Latina Girl botches her testimony, the prosecution will need to call her mother Maria to show her daughter's fragile state of mind after the alleged sexual assault.

My position is in the front row too, but on the other side of the gallery. Reynolds has a seat next to my husband at the defense table and takes a look at Grant's shirt, the awful tie, then glances back at me with a quick wink.

He and I are far from coconspirators. Part of me senses that he thinks Grant is guilty. Throughout the time spent prepping for trial, I heard the smug way he kept snagging on the point where Grant allowed the girl to sit at his table in the bar in the first place. Reynolds isn't particularly attractive, with a hard drinker's bulbous nose and a couple of wide folds at the belly. The only time a female approaches his table is to drop off the check.

We are all standing now as the jury assembles.

Courtrooms are strangely sacreligious in structure. The benches in the gallery appear more like pews, the judge presides above everyone else in the room like a priest at the altar. Those in judgment, the defendants, beg for mercy seated before the great seal of the State of California instead of a stained glass figure of Christ. The judge in Grant's case, a pleasant looking woman with thinning hair who I've tried a few cases in front of and won, tells us to be seated. In the same breath she nods to the prosecutor and requests that he call his next witness.

While the benches make settling sounds with all of our collective weight, I look down at my watch. I can't stand the sight of the Latina Girl, even if it's just the backside of her in that unseasonal cotton dress brushing past me as she makes her way down the aisle. With no physical evidence tying Grant to her, my husband must've used a condom, the State's entire case is riding on the Latina Girl's testimony. Although I'm sure she's been coached not to look this way, she does, at me. She's striking in that youthful way that could very well be blunted by the type of life she's about to lead as an adult. Something about me, the darkness of my eyes, makes her quickly change her mind. I, too, have never had a problem attracting men.

◆

Prosecutor: Please state for the court your name.

Witness: My name, Graciela Maria Lopez. L-O-P-E-Z.

Prosecutor: Miss Lopez, how old are you?

Witness: Eighteen. I mean, seventeen when, I... This happened, I was seventeen.

Prosecutor: Fine, fine. Can you provide the court with a little background on yourself? Are you a student?

Witness: (nods)

Prosecutor: No, Miss Lopez. You need to verbally answer the question.

Witness: I'm studying for big test so I won't go to school.

Prosecutor: You mean you're studying for the GED? The test that, if you pass, works instead of a high school diploma.

Witness: Yes.

Prosecutor: What is your family life like?

Witness: My father, he works hard at Las Cadenas.

Prosecutor: And that is?

Witness: Grocery store. He sweeps floors.

Prosecutor: And your father and mother are undocumented?

Witness: They live here eighteen years without getting caught. I was born here. But you say…

Prosecutor: Miss Lopez, the court isn't concerned with their status. We're only interested in what happened to you on the night of May 19 of this year. Do you have any other family members that live with you?

Witness: My brother Pedro. He's eleven. Uncle Antonio. He sends money back to Mexico for his family.

Prosecutor: Can you explain for the court what you were doing at Monty's Restaurant and Bar on the evening of May 19 of this year?

Witness: I was waiting, I was waiting for friend.

Prosecutor: And that friend would be?

Witness: Diego Marquez. He wash dishes in kitchen. He's like brother to me. Our families from Michoacán. Sometimes he walk me home or we go to Leena's house. She's our friend, too.

Prosecutor: I see. Your families, yours and Diego's are both from a certain part of Mexico?

Witness: Uh-huh.

Prosecutor: That's a yes?

Witness: Yes.

Prosecutor: Why, Miss Lopez, were you waiting for Diego Marquez in the bar?

Witness: I wasn't. That man, he stop me. I say I'm lost.

Prosecutor: What do you mean, you were lost?

Witness: I was looking for bathroom.

Prosecutor: Could you identify for the court if the man who stopped you in the bar is here now?

Witness: (pointing to the defense table) That man there in the gray suit. He stop me. He grab my wrist.

Prosecutor: Let the record reflect she's pointed to the defendant Grant Jacobsen. Did he say anything to you when he grabbed your wrist?

Witness: He laugh and say he want another drink.

Prosecutor: He thought you were a server?

Witness: A what?

Prosecutor: A waitress. He thought you were a cocktail waitress.

Witness: I guess.

Prosecutor: Did the defendant seem intoxicated to you?

Witness: I don't know.

Prosecutor: Drunk, Miss Lopez. Did the defendant seem drunk to you? Was he slurring his speech like he'd had too much alcohol?

Witness: (shaking her head) He say in perfect English to me what's my hurry. I real pretty. I should sit down. He gave me the rest of his drink.

Prosecutor: Did you inform the defendant that you were too young to be in the bar?

Witness: (Tears up and the first nub is debuted, trembling and pressed at her chapped lips) He say, "Shh... It's our little secret."

◆

BEHIND ME, I HEAR people in the gallery whispering, someone actually gasping out, "My God." The judge does nothing to silence them which speaks volumes to the jury. Never in our married lives has my husband acted condescending enough to put a finger to his mouth, to "shh" me like a child, but I feel it catch in my throat, how this crying girl in the cotton dress could be different. *He could've been a different man around the Latina Girl.*

There is the instinctual rush for me to flee. It's always been my way, to leave the scene, leave a relationship before I get hurt. But it's too late for any of that now. Loving Grant as deeply as I do makes me an unwitting accomplice to his crimes whether they're alleged or real. Every muscle in my body feels like dead weight. The gravity of the situation is that my husband is being annihilated by the Latina Girl's testimony.

I am not the only one sitting by to watch. During the time she's been on the stand there have been virtually no objections made by Grant's high-priced Century City attorney. Even if the judge overrules each and every one, the objection itself interrupts and throws off the line of questioning the witness and the prosecutor have spent hours upon hours rehearsing.

As for the jury, there are nine males among them a self-employed plumber, two electricians, a high school science teacher, and a few retirees. None of them have bothered to take any notes. A female librarian with a blunt bob is doing it for them, filling up her notebook with every word the Latina Girl utters. No doubt she's already announced herself the jury forewoman.

Two other women, somewhere in their thirties, soccer mom types with careful make-up and cared-for bodies, focus more on Grant than they do anyone else in the room, which could very well turn against him since he is not allowed to pay them any attention. Though it might help if he looked their way at least once, not something as forward as a smile, something he could get caught doing, but a quick glance to let the women know he's noticed them. That slight gesture coming from a defendant can go a long way in showing how unsure Grant is of himself, which is another way of looking innocent.

But this morning I'm already worn out by profiling the jury. The hell with what they'll think of me getting up, or Reynolds for that matter who I'm certain is behind the reason why my husband suddenly came up with the money to buy me a semester off from teaching. There is nothing more I'd rather do than teach my Criminal Justice classes at the state college nearby where I'm a full-time lecturer. Students and prep work would take my mind off the fact that my own husband might one day appear as a case study under sexual predators in the textbooks I cover.

I concentrate on taking even steps straight out of the courtroom, and I go so far as to click on my smart phone as if I have an urgent message that needs to be returned.

The Latina Girl's testimony has me rattled, shaking my belief in my husband yet again. *He stop me. He grab my wrist.* Ever since this whole thing started there has been no firm ground for me to stand on, no concrete evidence to prove my husband is telling me the truth other than his word, which used to be enough. Now I find myself listening to her, an eighteen-year-old who had no business being in a bar to begin with.

The hallway is vacant except for a few trash receptacles and a hunched over Mexican woman seated on a bench. She's knitting, two thick metal needles scraping against one another, a tongue of orange fabric trailing over her wrist.

She looks up like she's expecting me.

I recognize her eyes. As a potential witness, she is not allowed in the courtroom.

She knows me, too. Her fingers continue working with her focus still on me. They're the tough hands of a woman who doesn't own a dishwasher, who snaps clean sheets onto mattresses all day at her job as a housekeeper at a hotel near LAX, and hangs her own laundry out to dry.

"Lo siento por usted."

If I wasn't paying attention to her stare, I would think the woman was simply talking to herself. There was no specific anger in her voice, but it was a clear message directed at me.

Maybe she thinks she's being clever speaking to me in another language or maybe she simply doesn't know English. My job as a public defender taught me enough Spanish to get by all the way to Tijuana and back.

I point my finger at her and she stops knitting.

"Haga silencio."

What I say is no threat, but it's enough to spook the Latina Girl's mother up off the bench and into the restroom, abandoning her needles and yarn bag.

"Hey there, Counselor."

I turn.

It's Martin Durham, the honorable Superior Court judge Martin Durham, a man who would most likely be presiding over Grant's trial if he and I hadn't been previously romantically involved. Had he just been passing by to his own court, which was at the end of the hall, or was he waiting for me? Without the black robe he could be any well-suited lawyer or white-collar defendant. He can't seem to get over the fact that I quit being a public defender over a year ago in order to teach at a state college in the Valley. He can't seem to get over it because a large part of it, I'm sure he suspects, had everything to do with him.

"How are you holding up?"

I shrug. Given our history, I know not to give him any more than a simple gesture to read off me.

"I'm fine."

Martin murmurs something under his breath. With his dark blond hair and weathered surfer good looks, he appears like an imposter when he's seated at the bench of his courtroom in a black robe, a color photo of his hero Theodore Roosevelt on the wall behind him. He even has a long stick which resembles a policeman's baton nailed next to the photograph, which when I first met him I thought must've been a historical joke, though I eventually saw it was a real threat. He's holding up his own court now by being out here with me.

"Well, we all know you look fine, Ava. You're gorgeous."

The compliment makes me uncomfortable. From my friend and former assistant Monica who still works in the building, I've heard he's now dating a cute red headed court reporter.

"I tried..."

"I should get back," I say, cutting him off. "You know what it looks like if a wife isn't present in the courtroom to support her husband."

"What it looks like?" Martin studies the closed courtroom doors as if he can see right through the dense wood, at Grant, the man who took me away from him years before in the most unlikely of places. There must be a certain amount of justice Martin feels at his one-time romantic rival now a defendant accused of statutory rape, but at least, for once, he shows enough tact not to express it.

He matches his eyes with mine. What I know Martin always finds challenging about me is that he and I are in every way equals.

"You're more than just someone's wife, Ava. You're one of the best damn defense lawyers I've ever encountered in my courtroom." Martin holds open one of the doors for me, and it is a brief reprieve to hear his whisper in my ear overwhelm the Latina Girl's voice as she breaks down yet again on the witness stand. "That stupid prick in there *never* deserved you."

◆

THAT NIGHT, GRANT AND I pass back and forth a quick dinner of Chinese take-out, literally eating out of the boxes, something we never did before. We'd always bring out plates with a bottle of wine, typically red, no matter what color of meat, whether it was chicken or steak. Grant knows I prefer Merlot and he's poured us both a glass, but it's not to help us linger over a meal. It's to take the edge off the brutal day in court.

I've since refilled my glass. Married a little over three years, Grant and I typically were interested in hearing about each other's day, the inside jokes that somehow remained funny, the flirting that went on between us, verbal foreplay between two longtime lovers.

The stress of the trial, the threat of Grant spending a year long stint in prison, forever having to register as a sex offender, now turn our meals into silence.

Grant smiles uneasily as he scrapes his fork, getting the last of the Kung Pao Chicken in the carton.

"Want any more?"

He is a handsome man—big brown eyes and a full head of brown hair graying in all the right places with the nick-of-a-scar just above his left eyebrow earned one night from a dumb drinking game in college. But recently he is not the same person I'm used to facing at the dinner table. As soon as we came home from court he changed out of the suit and tie he's always been comfortable wearing given his profession as a stockbroker, into a white v-neck undershirt and jeans. A spot of sweet and sour sauce has stained the front of his shirt. It isn't like him not to notice.

I shake my head.

"You're sure?"

I nod.

"Because I'll give you all the chicken and take the shriveled-up soggy peppers for myself."

He's aware that all I've forced down is some steamed rice, and I've only eaten that not because I'm hungry but so the two glasses of Merlot I've consumed don't get me drunk.

I push my plate forward a little, giving in.

"Since you put it that way."

Grant and I are careful around each other because we have to be. Without sex as a means to diffuse an argument, he and I focus on being polite. What we feel for each other runs too deep. Marriage has done little but to ensure the inevitable certainty that the two of us share a passion so unrelenting we could destroy one another.

◆

LATER, LYING IN BED beside my husband, I go over the Latina Girl's testimony. The sobs were compelling, the nubs that came with it especially so, though she got a key piece of information wrong—she didn't get the color of the interior of Grant's Audi right. If I were cross-examining her I would've ripped holes in her story. I would be able to use that one mistake and transform her into a liar.

I would be able to get my husband off, guilty or not.

But Reynolds hadn't exploited that part of her direct testimony when he cross-examined her. Instead, all he was successful in doing was getting her to cry by rehashing the events straight out of the police report, which was far more damning. The attractive soccer mom groupies even shared a disapproving look with one another.

Grant is breathing a heavy rhythm next to me, though that could just be an act. I slide my hand near the warmth of his body, yet I stop short of touching him.

Sleep and sex. Our bedroom used to be the most uncomplicated room in the house. After news of the Latina Girl, it serves as a dark place to lay quiet with worry, to picture again and again the parked car, his unzipped pants, the crackle of a condom wrapper, the tactless juvenile moves of a horny teenage boy embodied in a forty-four-year-old man.

CHAPTER THREE

DEFENSE TACTICS

In the morning, I get up before Grant to avoid any conversation with him. A surprising part of the Latina Girl is between us now, her false testimony. Forgetting the color of the upholstery of her rapist's car is not exactly cause for an acquittal, but it is a big deal. Most victims remember their assaults in vivid detail, and yet she got this particular detail wrong. I know the implications if I point this fact out to him. Grant will not understand why I still have doubts of his innocence.

If Reynolds brings up the Latina Girl's slip-up in court it could backfire. The prosecution will likely claim she was too emotionally wrought, too worked up to remember something so insignificant. From my years trying cases, facts are often overwhelmed by feeling, especially among jurors who bring their own personal life experiences, their biases, and failures to deliberation. At one point the juror with the bob, who offered up during jury selection that she moonlighted as a Girl Scout leader, looked like she'd wanted to leap right out of the box and smother the Latina Girl in a maternal hug as the girl sorrowfully spat out her testimony. The human element has always been the biggest flaw in our judicial system.

And Grant had just sat there unmoved at the defense table, staring straight ahead, zoning out to anything his accuser said as if he was already convicted. Again and again, he twisted the gold wedding band on his finger, a gesture that a psychologist would have a field day with. In reality playing with his wedding band was a nervous habit, like biting nails or clearing the throat. Guilty or not, I didn't like seeing my husband give up on himself because it's the same as giving up on us, our marriage. With the prosecution resting yesterday following the Latina Girl's tearful testimony, the judge has requested the morning off, maybe for the jurors to collect themselves before the defense starts calling their witnesses this afternoon.

I stand looking at my husband belly down on the sheets, his face twisted to the side as if staying asleep all night had been a struggle. He is wearing a pair of black boxers, nothing else. The thought occurs to me of crawling back into bed, warming up to him, and slipping beneath his outstretched arm, pretending at least until the sunlight illuminates the room bright enough to wake him that things aren't what they are. He is the one I seek physical comfort from. Not having that connection with him feels like the numbing hurt of a phantom limb.

I try not to think that we might be cut off from each other's bodies for good. Sexual attraction is what brought Grant and I together in the first place. Then in time it's evolved into another kind of need, the need to physically be together whether it's lounging on the couch, bare feet to feet, reading parts of the newspaper on a slow Sunday morning, or an afternoon stocking up on produce and pasta at Trader Joe's. Sex, friendship and love, it all works for us in sustained unison.

I get dressed in our walk-in closet where I once seduced him in order to distract him from the dark mood I was in. It happened after a disturbing encounter I had in the parking lot at work not so long ago when I was still a public defender. Bad days came with the job. Grant stood at the doorway, listening to my flimsy excuse, then suddenly he let it go and made a grab for my half-naked body.

After I make coffee and down a cup, I leave a Post-It on the machine. *Meeting* is all I write. Grant will figure I'm headed to the university. Next semester, whether he's in prison or under this roof, I will be teaching my classes again. The house is quiet except for the sound of Grant moving around in our bedroom.

I leave the house before he gets the chance to be in the same room with me because, even though I've distorted the truth many times to get my former clients off, I've never been any good at lying to my husband.

◆

My father and I meet at Jerry's Deli on Ventura Boulevard because it's easier if we do. He still lives in the home where I watched him nearly get killed. The stain on the porch where he bled out was too deeply absorbed into the concrete and needed to be painted over with a stone gray color by a young male police officer, who came by and did it on his day off as if he was just following orders. Birthday cakes with candles blown out at the kitchen table, Christmas trees lit up in the family room, time spent sitting out on a porch swing with my mother, their hands loosely linked, watching the sun go down, these were all memories my father couldn't give up by moving away. Every time I go to the house I'm reminded why I lied to my mother during that first and only visit to the mental hospital she'd been put in indefinitely after her arrest. Even with the bullet she permanently forced into his spine, my father doesn't have it in his heart to stop loving her.

My father is already seated in a booth, his metal wheelchair folded, leaning against the side. Such a contraption looks misleading when you take in the rest of him. He has a head full of black hair that even in his late sixties stubbornly refuses to go white. His hands are tough and calloused, and his arms are taut from pushing the wheels. No electrical, top of the line model for my father. That kind of luxury would only make him go soft. As a former cop, my father is more than punctual. He's always at least ten minutes early. Two cups of coffee are on the table.

Although I'm right on time, I'm certain he's on his second cup by now.

The restaurant is just that, a restaurant, although it's called a deli. Across from the cashier is a glass bakery case with towering chocolate cakes, tiramisu, lemon meringue, and banana cream pies. In the dining area, two wall TVs play the same local morning news program. A ditzy weather woman over-laughs at something the male anchor has said. Thankfully, the sound is turned down.

"Kitsoli" my father says, the Greek word for "little girl" he's called me ever since I could walk. The fact that I'm well into my thirties means nothing.

I smile as I sit down across from him.

My father assesses me, my forced cheer. I'm running on only a few hours sleep and I imagine it shows.

"You've lost weight."

"Just a little." He hasn't seen me for a couple weeks, and in that time my clothes have become so loose I've taken to safety pinning them inside the waistline.

"Order a real breakfast, Kitsoli. I don't want you picking at a side of fruit."

The waitress is quick to come by and I order an egg white omelet and confuse her by saying I want it with greasy hash browns. Not even my meals make sense anymore.

My father leans forward. "I got a call the other day." He looks away from me through the slits in the blinds. A public bus has stopped right outside and a teenage girl with bright blonde hair and a backpack is unlatching her bike off the front grill. She could be the Latina Girl's age.

He faces me again. "Some goddamn reporter, or is it a blogger? I don't know what the hell you call them in this day and age."

"I'm sorry, Dad." Since the trial began I've been approached by a journalist from the *LA Times* who did a bit piece on Grant that fortunately appeared in the middle of the paper. A scandal is only as good as the red meat on its bones. With a gag order put in place by the judge, the sensationalism of the story has so far been snuffed out. No one who is part of the proceedings is allowed to comment until the trial is over.

"I wasn't expecting anyone to track you down."

"No, not about Grant. It was about your mother."

There isn't a place my father and I frequent that I don't envision her popping back into our lives. Sometimes she is young and beautiful—a slash of red lipstick and her dark hair pinned back in glamorous curls. Other times her lips are cracked, her hair gray and unwashed. She is ageless, sometimes faceless, a haunting image that never takes definitive form. The truth is neither of us knows whether she is dead or alive. My father finds hope in this, while I only feel dread.

I'm careful in what I say next.

"What about her?"

"Apparently, what's been long buried in a police file now resurfaces on the Internet. There isn't much to find that's public record. Most of her case has been sealed. I just thought you should know if you get a call."

For a while I talk about the new semester starting soon, the specialized California Law class I'll be teaching, anything to steer clear of the subject of my mother or Grant's trial.

The waitress brings our food and my father and I just work on our breakfast. I'm actually sampling everything on my plate, the egg omelet and the hash browns, unlike last night.

"When are closing arguments, Kitsoli?"

"Considering Grant is probably the only witness on the defense list, probably tomorrow."

"What kind of defense lawyer only calls his defendant as a witness?"

I shake my head.

"One who's convinced that he will show the prosecution has no case. It's a big gamble, especially with this jury."

"I'll be there."

"Dad," I say, "I already told you before. There's really no point."

We both know what he's offering up—the use of his physical handicap to steal sympathy away from the young victim and her immigrant family. Look at the defendant's father-in-law, willing to wheel his way to court to show his support. My father has remained silent on Grant's guilt or innocence, which says more than if he told me outright that he thought Grant did it. He thinks his own son-in-law is capable of statutory rape.

"Not another word, Kitsoli," my father repeats. "You need to keep eating."

◆

MY FATHER IS DRIVING out of the parking lot when Grant calls my cell. I'm seated in my Volkswagon Passat, the engine idling. The needle of the gas gauge is in the red.

"V," he says. "I would've called earlier, but I forgot you changed your number again. I had to scroll through recent calls to find it."

I think of something to say.

"I'm with my dad."

"How is he?"

"Good. He's coming tomorrow for closing arguments."

"It might be a day after tomorrow. Reynolds thinks Margaret should testify. I said I thought I'd run it by you first."

My husband isn't asking me as his second wife whether it's okay if his first wife testifies in his defense. He's asking me as a lawyer, which means he might have second thoughts. By adding a last minute witness it shows Reynolds is worried they're losing the case.

"I think it would be a mistake."

Grant lets out a quick burst of breath. This is not what he wants to hear. He's running out of opportunities, out of people to paint himself as a good person in front of the jury.

"Why not? She and I had a relatively easy divorce. No bloodshed, at least. She could vouch for my character, the fact that I gave her everything."

"Everything but your fidelity," I point out.

It is quiet on the other end, the noiselessness of my husband licking his wounds. My intention isn't to insult him.

"Grant, you cheated on her with me, remember? It's the same reason why I can't be called as a witness because all of it will be dug up. How you left. Why." I take a deep breath, but it doesn't help. "I don't understand what the hell is wrong with your lawyer, why he wants to watch one of your wives bury you in open court."

"Jesus, V. Ex-wife. You make me sound like a goddamn polygamist."

Grant is good with numbers. He's good with stocks. He's best at making money, but he's worthless when it comes to thinking things through, utilizing a little common sense.

"I'm just telling you what the jury will see, Grant. And if they don't see it on their own, then Daniels will definitely point it out for them on cross."

"Fine. I'll have Reynolds nix the idea. Guess it's only me then." He chuckles. "I'm my only fucking witness."

The weakness in his voice, bordering on blame, annoys me. I'm not the one who put him on trial for statutory rape. He did it to himself by not chasing that Latina Girl away. Instead, he let her have a seat at his booth, let her share his Stoli on the rocks.

"Are you on your way over? Court starts in an hour."

A good-looking man pulls up alongside me in a gray Mercedes. He's younger, or trying to be, with longish hair in the back, floppy hair in the front. His smile looks too perfect, like veneers. His mouth must smell self-consciously of mouthwash. Maybe an actor or a producer. The movie studios are only a couple miles away from here. Even with my husband on the line, all this man sees is that technically I am alone. Women tend to see so much more. We check for a wedding band, a tan line on that ring finger, evidence that he is already committed. We foolishly look for permanence even in a one night stand.

Flirting back with a stranger, leaping ahead to a five star hotel room with the works—chilled champagne and a steaming shower won't change the fact my husband is most likely going to prison for up to a year. The thought of the Mercedes man's mouth, the sureness of his antiseptic breath, suddenly repulses me.

Grant doesn't try so hard. He simply brushes his teeth.

"V? You'll be there?"

I turn away from the guy in the Mercedes and notice the warning light on the dashboard. My car is running on empty, but Ventura Boulevard is teeming with gas stations. I'm already reversing before the man in the Mercedes realizes he's lost his shot at late-morning sex with an emotional basket case in the parking lot of Jerry's Deli.

"Yes," I finally tell my husband. "Where else would I be?"

CHAPTER FOUR

DISPUTABLE FACTS

Grant is right to sound nervous. For nearly two weeks the prosecution called its list of witnesses: the double-chinned sergeant who took the Latina Girl's police report *eleven hours* after Grant supposedly assaulted her in an empty parking lot. The rank, the uniform, the bulging bullet proof vest underneath and his disinterested demeanor gave the cop as well as the Latina Girl a certain level of credibility. Here was a man who didn't bother breaking out a ballpoint pen and the proper forms unless he felt the Latina Girl had a serious claim, unless he thought she indeed might be a victim.

Then came the bitter-faced female medical examiner who admitted to the fruitless rape kit that provided no

DNA evidence, not even any helpful scrapings of Grant's skin found under the Latina Girl's fingernails.

Her scientific answer?

Victims oftentimes take showers before braving the police because they feel so unclean. Ivory soap and a loofah sponge were the real reasons why the physical evidence was indeed a wash.

The juror with the bob haircut wrote so furiously in her notepad I thought she'd rip the page as if supposition from the mouth of a medical examiner somehow made it a bonafide fact.

Another damaging witness was Diego Marquez. He is the Latina Girl's friend, a dishwasher at Monty's, who, being a couple years older than her, managed to be one of the strongest witnesses. He spoke of Grant's alleged victim like she was a little sister, recounting that he'd danced with her at her quinceanera when she turned fifteen, the fancy pink dress and tiara she wore, the extra sweet pan de salvo served for dessert. Dressed in black pants, a black button down shirt, and his black hair slicked back in a ponytail, he was respectful to the judge, articulate and short with his answers. He came off as sincere. If Diego didn't have fifteen minutes left on his shift, he would've stopped the Latina Girl from taking Grant up on his offer to drive her home.

My husband having one foot already in a prison cell halfway through his trial isn't all Reynolds's fault. Typically, circumstantial cases fall apart right about now, and I'm assuming Reynolds is counting on it. Jurors tend to demand an absurd amount of proof to find someone guilty. Whenever this subject gets brought up in one of my classes, I point out that famous baseball player whose blood trail led from his butchered girlfriend's apartment, to his Porsche, all the way into his own home, or the young mother in Oregon who was acquitted for the murder of her son even though she failed to report the little boy missing for weeks and hosted a jewelry party in her condo that witnesses testified reeked of a dead body.

Not only is race involved in Grant's case, so is economic disparity, a young attractive Latina girl from South LA and a much wealthier, also attractive, middle aged white man shacked up with his second wife in Studio City. By Grant looking like he does and living the life he's led, he's proven he already has it all, so it somehow makes sense that he's still greedily grabbing for more. *He stop me. He grab my wrist.*

It is not just the State of California against Grant Jacobsen.

It is naïvety vs. ego.

It is why my husband will be found guilty whether he forced himself on a seventeen-year-old girl or not.

Grant greets me at the elevator doors on the third floor as they slide apart, my image in the reflective steel disappearing with his. The eagerness in his eyes at the sight of me stings me with sympathy, and I feel myself soften some to the vulnerability he's exposed. My husband didn't know if I was telling him the truth that I'd show up to court in time for his testimony. His uncertainty puts me on surer footing; I have not lost as much ground now that I am no longer the only one in this relationship with trust issues.

I check my watch. Five minutes before one. Sometimes this judge arrives early from lunch and if she does then court is expected to start. Odds are she is already on the bench, glaring down at Reynolds who sits fixed between her judicial cross-hairs at the defense table without his client. Defense lawyers aren't popular with judges to begin with. They make too much money, not to mention the mockery they make of the law, sobering murder confessions thrown out because a suspect claims he was drunk or had snorted too much coke and didn't fully understand his Miranda Rights, the miniscule mistakes in the routine collection of evidence at a crime scene that defense lawyers blow out of proportion in front of jurors who pride themselves as expert investigators themselves from the cop shows they watch on TV.

"Shouldn't you be in there?" I ask.

"Not without you." Grant touches the middle of my back, the way he does when we enter a restaurant or find our seats at an outdoor concert at the Hollywood Bowl. The first real gesture from him that reminds me of our married life before his arrest. No more public hand holding.

The charade is officially off.

At the double doors to the courtroom, one of Reynolds's assistants keeps an eye on Grant. He is tall and stringy, still in law school, maybe even prelaw. A smart phone is wedged between his hands and his thumbs begin to frantically tap out a message, most likely to his boss. *The wife finally showed up.* Before Grant and I reach the doors, I stop.

"She got it wrong," I say.

"What?"

"The color of your car upholstery. You should let Reynolds know."

Grant nods, startled by what I've blurted out. He is a man who thinks first, then speaks. What I've just shared with him is important to his case. It could possibly impeach the prosecution's star witness. And yet he must also be trying to figure out why I'm telling him now, over twenty-four hours after her testimony. Was his own wife contemplating sabotaging his chances at an acquittal?

Inside, the gallery is fuller than before with strange faces I don't recognize. Through word of mouth, my husband's case is gaining popularity with pathetic court watchers who have nothing better to do than be a spectator at someone else's legal drama. As I assumed, the judge is out of her chamber, seated at the bench, her thin hair freshly brushed. She remains silent, sizing up the growing gallery. The Latina Girl's mother is in the first row next to her husband. In a drab gray hotel uniform, an untidy bun, she's just come off her shift. When Grant gets up from the defense table, the Latina Girl's parents lean into each other, whispering.

I can guess the ugly things they're saying about my husband. How *can* they sit so calmly in a room with their daughter's rapist?

Grant raises his right hand to be sworn in.

For close to an hour, Reynolds walks Grant through his direct testimony, why Grant chose to have a drink at Monty's Restaurant and Bar that afternoon. He'd had a little work left to do, but given it was a Friday, he no longer felt like staying at the office to complete it. None of the jurors are taking notes. Grant has the two busty soccer moms' rapt attention but they could be mentally checked out, drafting in their minds something as innocuous as a grocery list or maybe, if they already figure he's guilty, how they'll phrase their first letter to him in prison. As for the men on the jury, most of them have their arms folded at their chests, simply listening.

The plumber glances again and again in my direction. His hair is white, his face sunburned, though the majority of his time is spent under the cool cover of a leaky sink. From jury selection I remember he is divorced, runs his own business, about ready to retire. He leans forward in his chair, wondering why Grant wasn't home with me. The suspicion in his eyes is a cinch to read. It's where the lonely plumber would be if he had a reliable woman, not getting smashed like a single guy at some crowded bar.

A few jurors shift and straighten after Reynolds completes his questioning and settles back at the defense table.

Grant is no intimidated defendant, anxiously awaiting cross-examination by Daniels who is slowly making his way over to the jury box. Instead, Grant's attention is drawn to the back of the courtroom as if he's spotted a person he hadn't anticipated to see here.

I turn. The doors are closing. Whoever it was has just left, and I imagine Grant probably wishes he could leave, too.

Daniels will question Grant mere inches from the jury box, a tactic some lawyers do to encourage the jurors to feel he is one with them, they're all on the same side.

I never pulled that ploy in court because it always seemed too obvious. Daniels's strategy fails, at least with the plumber, because he's now aligned back in his seat, his arms folded at his chest like the other male jury members, creating distance.

◆

Prosecutor: Please explain to the court where you were on the evening of May 19 of this year.

Defendant: I was home with my wife that evening.

Prosecutor: Late afternoon, then. Sir, will you please answer the question—were you at Monty's Restaurant and Bar on May 19 of this year?

Defendant: Yes, I was there around four, having a drink, going over some numbers.

Prosecutor: Were you seated in the restaurant area or in the bar?

Defendant: I think it's already been established I was in the bar.

Prosecutor: What, sir, were you drinking?

Defendant: A Stoli on the rocks.

Prosecutor: How many drinks did you consume?

Defendant: One.

Prosecutor: You're claiming you only had one?

Defendant: Yes. I didn't get a chance to drink the second Stoli I ordered.

Prosecutor: Were you intoxicated?

Defendant: Obviously, no. One Stoli on the rocks couldn't even get a housewife drunk.

I grit my teeth to the point of provoking a headache. Stupid, stupid, stupid of him to insult housewives in general when two of them are in the jury box about to decide his fate. Not to mention these two stay-at-home soccer moms, practically Grant's groupies, probably could hold their liquor better than any man. They probably pound shots of tequila while playing Bunco or lightening the dark roots in each other's hair. Maybe Grant senses the destructive sexual vibe off them and so he's trying to ingratiate himself with the men on the jury like the plumber. All he needs is one vote of not guilty for a hung jury.

Prosecutor: How did you meet Miss Lopez?

Defendant: She came up to my table. I was working and hadn't noticed she'd sat down and taken my drink.

Prosecutor: That would be your second Stoli on the rocks?

Defendant: Yes.

Prosecutor: It is your testimony that she approached your table. You did not stop her.

Defendant: Like I said, I had no idea she'd even sat down.

Prosecutor: Do you find Miss Lopez attractive?

Defendant: I find her young. Too young.

Prosecutor: Please explain to the court what you mean by "too young?"

Defendant: It means anyone can see she's underage. Even with all the make-up she had on that day. She had no reason to be in that bar. She should've been carded and thrown out.

Prosecutor: So you are not disputing that the two of you sat at a table together.

Defendant: I was uncomfortable. I wasn't sure how to ask her to leave.

Prosecutor: That would be a yes or no answer, sir. Were you and Miss Lopez seated at a table together in Monty's Bar?

Defendant: Briefly, yes.

Prosecutor: Did you offer Miss Lopez a ride home?

Defendant: No.

Prosecutor: Did you drive Miss Lopez to a parking lot of a nearby warehouse and force Miss Lopez to perform oral sex on you?

Defendant: No.

Prosecutor: Did you vaginally rape Miss Lopez using a condom?

Defendant: Jesus Christ.

Prosecutor: Please answer yes or no.

Defendant: No. I never touched that girl. She's lying. Listen to her. She's making it all up, everything, it's all bullshit. Even her accent comes and goes.

Prosecutor: Her accent comes and goes? Is that what you just said?

Defendant: Yes.

Prosecutor: In your own words, Miss Lopez's accent comes and goes. I suppose, according to you, that would mean her tears at the sight of you are fake, too. (Glances toward the judge) Withdrawn, your honor. No further questions at this time.

CHAPTER FIVE

FINAL REMARKS

The Latina Girl shows up for closing arguments, her hair in a cheerleader's ponytail. I don't see what clothing she has on because she's sandwiched between her parents. I only see that exposed slender neck and a few thin baby hairs. Occasionally, while Daniels speaks of her testimony, of how my husband hit the automatic locks to his Audi when she tried to open the passenger door and get out, she dabs at her eyes with a white handkerchief. Not a Kleenex. An old fashioned handkerchief, a sympathy prop, something only British valets still use.

The Botox soccer moms are glammed up for today, one last ditch effort to knock Grant right out of the defendant's chair before they head into the deliberating

room and convict him. One of the women has cut a
new line of bangs, wearing a tight off-the-shoulder pink
sweater that makes her breasts resemble a pair of Easter
eggs. Her almost twin is in a red halter-top, fit more for
clubbing than a courtroom. *See what you'll be thinking
about while lying on a prison cot with one hand on your
groin.* If they had any clue, they'd see by my long dark
curly hair and the Latina Girl's black ponytail, Grant is
not much into blondes, natural or out of the bottle. The
comparison I find between myself and the Latina Girl
makes me feel nauseous.

During the break before Reynolds begins his closing
argument, my father is wheeled into court by my friend
and former assistant, Monica. She rolls him straight
down the aisle and locks the chair right beside me. His
muscled arms are concealed in a seasonally correct long
sleeve flannel shirt. The temperature is a little cool for
LA, in the low sixties. Christmas is, after all, only a couple
weeks away.

Monica is a tough girl with short curly hair and an
iron jaw line, but her eyes are giving her away, like she
could start crying.

"Good luck," she mouths to me, ignoring Grant who
turns and smiles hopefully in her direction.

The scene is a sad one if you were her. She was a
witness, along with her live-in girlfriend, at Grant's and
my wedding in Big Sur. It is her signature on our marriage
certificate. She was also dead set against me quitting the
public defender's office.

It is my fault she doesn't know any better. I've never told her or anyone else for that matter why I really had to stop practicing law and teach it instead. Monica, Grant, and my father assume the obvious—my conscience finally got to me. An internal fatigue from speaking day in and day out for heartless thugs who do everything from hold up the corner convenience store, blasting a bullet into the cashier's chest because he isn't giving the gun man the bills out of the drawers fast enough to the car jacker who stuns an elderly driver into suffering a fatal heart attack as he's roughly pulled from his car at a stoplight. My duty was to negotiate lighter sentences for hardcore felons so that they may get out of prison sooner to repeat the same crimes.

But in actuality, I only represented a few criminals who showed no signs of remorse. In fact I loved my job. Walking away from it is one of the hardest things I've ever done. Being a public defender is why I became a lawyer. Some might mistakenly conclude that a career in law is my adult way of coping with a childhood where I witnessed the unthinkable—my mother attempting to kill my father—and maybe that's true to some degree. I've wanted to defend *real victims* of the court system. My mother, given she's successfully been on the lam for decades, most definitely is not one of them. I wanted to defend people who deserved my help, who lived life on the margins and would be guaranteed prison instead of probation simply because they couldn't afford good counsel. So many of my young clients came from broken homes, meth head parents who sent them out on drug runs, and in turn got popped by the cops for it. That's how they started doing dope to begin with, bumming a line or two off their mother or father's stash. I've defended gang kids as young as fourteen who joined gangs for protection. They joined gangs to feel part of a family who for once had their back. These are the types of people who deserve a second chance, not a woman who flew into a murderous rage because her husband dared to try and leave her.

The truth behind why I resigned remains where it needs to be, between myself and the man who confronted me with it: Judge Martin Durham.

◆

IN HIS CLOSING ARGUMENTS, Reynolds does what he can to stop the bleeding after Grant's damaging cross-examination. Grant's anger on the stand could've been read one way: a husband who loves his wife more than anything and just wants this hell to be over so he can return to his life with her. That is, before his accusation that the Latina Girl's accent isn't real. In the eyes of the jury, what Grant said runs the risk of overwhelming his entire testimony, making him sound like a racist, a guilty man who is lashing out because he's been caught of his crimes.

For his part, Grant sits at the defense table in a navy blue suit, a silver tie, one of his favorite work outfits he picked out this morning without my help. Neither one of us cares anymore how cold he may look to the jury.

Somewhere in the second half hour of his closing arguments Reynolds finds a way to mention that the Latina Girl didn't get the color of Grant's upholstery right.

"Ladies and gentlemen of the jury," Reynolds says loudly, hitching up his belt. I imagine he's had to buy a bigger one since he began prepping for Grant's trial.

"The most chilling fact about this case is the fact there are no facts in this case." He stands a couple of safe feet away from the jury box and points back toward Grant while still maintaining eye contact with the jurors. "Here sits a man that could very well be convicted with no physical evidence, and only from the words of his alleged victim, whom you already have heard has a faulty memory."

Unlike his reckless client, Reynolds chooses his words carefully. He comes as close as possible to calling the Latina Girl a liar without offending the jurors who sympathize with and actually believe her.

In his rebuttal, Daniels pounces on the word "chilling" and improvises during his second at bat with the jury.

"I'll tell you what would be *chilling*, members of the jury. What would be *very chilling* is if you don't believe the words of Graciela Maria Lopez." He stretches out the syllables of her name for full ethnic impact, a racist in his own right who has blatantly used her brown color to help rest his case.

◆

GRANT AND I DON'T wait anywhere near the courthouse
for the verdict. We decide to head home. My father
turns down an offer to come with us. Near the elevators,
he shakes Grant's hand. It's the closest he's come to
supporting his son-in-law since he found out about
Grant's arrest. His face is grim. My father's a Greek who's
doing his best to hold back.

"You understand I'm here for my daughter?"

Grant nods, though his disappoint shows. He's
always respected my father, his strength, the fact he's
taken a bullet and somehow survived.

None of Grant's family is aware of his legal troubles.
He likes to say he doesn't keep in close contact with his
parents because they sided with his first wife Margaret
during the divorce, a fairly quick proceeding that still
managed to outlast their lightning fast marriage. But
he kept his family at arm's length, three thousand miles
away on the East Coast even before then. My husband
is a person with the unnatural capability of cutting a
loved one out of his life without any real explanation or
sentiment. A casual decision like waking up one morning
and deciding he no longer would pour cream in his coffee.

My father rolls up his sleeves. Veins surface on his
forearms, Hulk style, as he grips the wheels. It must've
killed him to allow himself to be pushed anywhere. It
must've been just as hard for him to reach a hand out
to Grant.

He loves me that much.

◆

ON THE WAY HOME, signs of Christmas bombard us on every block. Silver garlands wind up lamp posts, red ribbon wreaths hang off practically every shop door, and a giant inflatable snowman bends in the breeze at a Honda dealership.

Grant and I haven't bothered with a tree this year. Since we've been together, it's become our tradition to spend hours going from lot to lot picking out a Douglas fir as tall as him, if not taller. Last year we ended up all the way in Beverly Hills before we found the right one with soft green needles for branches and a long stem at the top fit for a gold star. We were particular in how we decorated it, too, cleanly, with only red bulbs and white lights like a stock Christmas tree you'd find in the window of a department store.

This year we have no presents either. Between shuttling back and forth to the courthouse there is no time for anything but a quick stop to Starbucks in the morning and takeout on the way home for dinner.

I'm seated in the passenger seat of his Audi, the crime scene, if you are to believe the Latina Girl. My mind is stuck on the fact that she and I are both brunettes. Technically it's not much, just hair color, but it's something at this moment while the jury is now in deliberation that I can't seem to let go of.

At home, I am on my laptop on the couch, working on the syllabus for my California Law class next semester, trying not to glance down at the clock in the right corner of my computer screen. So far the jury has been deliberating for one and a half hours.

Grant is sitting on the hardwood floor in front of me, his legs crossed, still wearing his dress shoes. We have come home to relax, but even in our most familiar place both of us remain on edge. On the coffee table, two mugs of hot tea have grown cold. Grant is on his tablet, focusing hard on the screen.

"If I'm sentenced, V, when would I have to start serving my time?"

"Grant."

"No, V. Please, just tell me when."

"Probably in a couple weeks. Why?"

Grant starts tapping away on the keyboard.

"It's settled then."

"What is?"

"Christmas is a bust, so let me take you somewhere, give you a going away present." Grant laughs, though he knows what he's saying is far from funny. "Except it's me who's technically going away for the next twelve months."

I touch his shoulder, grateful his back is to me. He doesn't need to see that I believe what he says is true—he will be convicted, and I will lose him.

"You don't know that."

Grant takes my hand and encircles my wrist, stroking the inside of my forearm with his thumb, a motion that tends to calm him down more than me.

"Yeah, V, I do."

A colorful hotel with palm trees, white cabanas, and a tear drop pool takes up his computer screen, and for a moment I warm along with him to the thought of this false paradise. Palm Springs, a place within the boundaries of his bond agreement.

The phone rings.

It is a bad sign. It is a bad sound. It must be Reynolds calling to say the jury has come back with a verdict already, in under two hours.

CHAPTER SIX

AMBUSH

Some might call it callous of me not to be inside the courtroom when the verdict is read. My support for my husband has somehow waned. The fact is I'm not sure if I can compose myself. There are leaks in my resolve. I will not give the Botox pair or the female librarian the satisfaction of witnessing my grief as my husband officially turns from defendant to convicted felon. Three years of impassioned married life eclipsed by a disputed thirty-minute car ride with a seventeen-year-old Latina Girl. A car ride that Grant denies ever took place. No long strand of black hair found on the floorboard. She didn't even remember the color of the car seat where she was attacked. *He stop me. He grab my wrist.*

The Latina Girl's words echo over and over again in my head like the popping sound of a gunshot the night my mother took aim at my father. Why is it that the men I love are always threatened to be taken from me by other women?

Inside the restroom of the courthouse, I run cold water on the whites of my wrists. I avoid my reflection in the mirror.

The reality is stark. I've covered countless rape cases in my classes, how rare they are because most victims don't want their past sexual experiences exposed to the court and exploited by the defense. Many of these women never recover from the trauma of testifying. It's demoralizing, it's shameful. It sometimes feels, for them, even worse than the actual rape. However, when these cases are tried, the odds shift in the female victim's favor, especially if she's young. The woman is brave just for stepping forward onto that witness stand. Whether or not she is actually telling the truth isn't the point anymore. It's her truth and that's all that matters.

That part is what scares me. Even with a recent birthday, the Latina Girl is only eighteen.

Jurors for Grant's case spent less than two hours to reach their decision, which means their minds had already been made up before they entered the deliberation room.

A woman in her fifties squeaks and shuffles out of the bathroom stall, leaving the trailing sound of a flushing toilet. She is awkwardly overweight for her age, carrying it all in her hips and mid-section, pregnancy pounds without the baby.

"Man," she says, "my dogs are barking."

The running shoes on her feet paired with a blouse and a knee length skirt don't fit. This is Southern California, not urban Manhattan or Philadelphia where people walk miles upon miles from subways to work. This is LA. We don't do mass transit. We'll drive down to the corner market in our cars.

I don't answer her.

Her movements seem self-conscious, out of sync, because she knows I'm watching. She dangles her hands in the sink without turning on the water. Her hair is cropped short and her cheeks are rashy like she's always overheated, straining for breath, a heart attack waiting to happen. Through the mirror her watery blue eyes flash then shrink at me with pinpoint recognition.

Suddenly, I remember my father's warning at breakfast the other day about a blogger asking him questions. He thought maybe I'd be next. Has this woman been hiding in a stall waiting to ambush me?

I run my wet hands through my hair, a faster way of drying them than if I waited for the hot air of the hand blower. Then I take a step for the door.

There's the irritating noise of her shoes on the tile floor again. The tennis shoes are for catching up with people. She's not about to let me get away.

"Will you divorce him, Mrs. Jacobsen, now that your husband is a registered sex offender?"

The words strike me in my place.

So the verdict is out.

There is no more hope for a hung jury. The lawyer in me read the jury, predicted this very outcome right after jury selection was completed, and yet in the back of my mind the wife in me silently bet on the chance of a solitary holdout—that single plumber in the first row who couldn't stop staring at me, that he, in the end, wouldn't leave me to live my life all alone, too.

But the words of an eighteen-year-old hold more weight than the absence of any physical evidence.

My husband is a statutory rapist, period. I don't know which is worse, hearing it announced to a crowded courtroom by the thin haired judge, or here inside the women's restroom from the mouth of a red faced woman tasteless enough to pair a knee length skirt with running shoes.

"Mrs. Jacobsen."

I turn.

"It's Ava."

Stupidly this woman assumes she's making headway with me. Revealing my first name is a sign she has me right where she wants me, about to get the big interview with the wife of a convicted statutory rapist. Maybe she'll even get it posted on a real news site like the *Huffington Post*. She pulls out her smart phone covered in an obnoxious polka dotted Lady Bug case.

I try not to smile at how wrong she is. The situation is this—she and I are the only two in here.

"I'm guessing you know a lot more about me than just my last name."

The woman nods, pressing down on the face of her phone, my every word now being recorded.

"I know about your mother being incarcerated."

"She was sent to a hospital for the mentally ill. You should always get your facts straight."

"Yes, yes, I also know how she…"

"*I know* how you called my father," I say talking over her. "How do you think that makes me feel? Every day of his life he's reminded of the bullet that woman buried in his back. If you were his daughter, wouldn't you think he's endured enough?"

The woman isn't sure how to respond and I use her cluelessness to my advantage. I grab the phone right out of her hand and within seconds the cover is ripped off and her phone is sinking to the bottom of a toilet bowl, third stall from the door.

"You bitch," the blogger cries out, unoriginally. She must be a terrible writer if she can't think on her feet of a cleverer comeback.

Just then someone enters the restroom, a courthouse worker with a stack of manila files she irresponsibly places on a sink so they won't rest on the unsanitary bathroom floor. She enters the stall furthest away from us, then locks the door, her bare ankles and black patent leather low pumps showing from underneath.

The blogger dashes toward the toilet, kneeling over the porcelain as if she's about to be sick. Her heels, in bright pink socks, slip out of her running shoes as she drives her hand into the water to fish out her phone.

From behind, I lean over her, holding down her flabby arm that tenses up, that practically trembles in anger or fear. When I press down harder against her wrist, I feel her pulse come to life under my thumb. Overpowering her is that easy, and I keep her hand submerged in the toilet so she understands I'm serious. Never have I lost control in this way. I recognize my physical reaction for what it is—something my mother would do. Yet I still don't let up. The blogger's breath comes out of her in low broken gasps. She wants to scream for help, I can sense it, but in her current state she can't form the word. That woman with the files is less than fifteen feet away locked in another stall. She may as well be fifteen miles from here. My other hand moves behind the blogger's thick clammy neck.

"You call my father again," I whisper, "and you'll lose something more valuable than your phone."

Outside in the courtroom hall I spot my husband huddled with Reynolds, the prelaw student keeping guard to ward off any interruptions. With both suits blocking him, Grant won't be able to notice me standing here even if he tries. He won't take me in his arms like I desperately need him to and tell me everything is going to be all right. *We'll be all right.* Right now, Reynolds is doing everything to reassure his client with promises of a swift appeal, a plea for a lighter sentence, the common rhetoric of a defense already lost.

Martin comes at me in his black robe that drapes around him like some kind of gothic villain. I'm guessing he's baffled everyone in his courtroom by abandoning a live trial that cannot continue without the judge.

"I just heard," he says. His voice is gentle, like he's about to offer me a back rub. "Is there anything I can do?"

I jab a finger toward the restroom door, all nerves and anguish.

"You can have security throw out the badly dressed woman who's about to walk out of there."

Martin is a man who relishes any reason to exercise his power. When it comes to me, he's already proved he'll do just about anything.

"Done."

CHAPTER SEVEN

CRIME OF PASSION

Before I was encouraged by my husband and his lawyer to take a semester off for Grant's trial, I'd used a popular case study in my lecture. Class discussion that day was on the definition of a sudden passion killing. The unlikely couple I chose, Clara and David, each had a degree in dentistry. I outlined to the class how they met in dental school and seemed from the very beginning to be the perfect pair. David eventually studied orthodontics, as well. They functioned as marital partners and business partners. Together they built up thriving practices in the suburbs of Houston, Texas.

"They further lived the cliché," I said to my students, "by getting married on Valentine's Day."

Because it was the last weeks of the semester with the lengthy Scantron final looming, the lecture hall was packed with a good hundred students. Three tiny fold out desks attached to each theater chair were cluttered with laptops, travel mugs of coffee, cans of energy drinks, notebooks and pens.

A smart-ass guy seated in the front row grinned like he agreed with me. He was one of those irritating types, part of the slim pack of the biologically fortunate like Grant who had it all—intelligence, wit, and looks. A slacker of sorts in baggy jeans and a vintage black Rolling Stone T-shirt, he slouched in his chair, the posture of the disinterested, yet followed my every word. No doubt a bright political career or a flashy job as a defense lawyer was in his future. Only in his early twenties, he'd probably already loved and left a trail of devastated young dorm girls in his wake.

"Doomed to fail then, Professor Nicoli. Doomed to fail."

"And why is that?"

The smart-ass lifted his palms, face up. He had a small black tattoo of an ace like you'd find in a deck of cards inked on the inside of his wrist. A real ace up his sleeve, I guessed.

"They were trying too hard at establishing romance. A red flag if you ask me."

Most of the females in the room laughed, charmed by anything that came out of his mouth, negative or positive, if it dealt with male and female relationships.

"You might have a point," I said. "Sameness is not the same as love, and David soon grew tired of his wife who in many respects was the mirror image of himself."

My students were listening, though not many were bothering to take notes. I hadn't gotten to the legal aspects of the case yet so there was no need.

"David began an affair with a woman who was not his equal. She was an employee, not a fellow employer. His lover was a divorced dental hygienist with two kids of her own. She needed David in a financial way that his wife didn't. Once Clara found out, she confronted her husband. Not only did David admit to the affair, but he seemingly took perverse pleasure in describing his relationship with the hygienist in explicit sexual detail."

"I got it, why the guy was acting like such a douche."

The smart-ass didn't bother to raise his hand this time. "Maybe he needed to make his wife, for once, feel powerless."

A sorority girl in the back frowned. She bucked the average stereotype of a pretty dumb blonde. Her GPA was a 4.0. She had big plans of moving to Manhattan and weaseling her way in at the bottom of the corporate ladder at a lucrative global powerhouse like Morgan Stanley.

"I've read about this case before. Leaving the marriage was not an option for Clara. How could she? David was not just her husband. He was in her DNA."

The smart-ass turned to check her out. He shook his head. I continued on about how Clara insisted her husband break off the affair.

"But as with any spouse caught cheating, can his or her word ever be trusted again?"

My words as I said them out loud personally held new meaning and brought cheating on a spouse to a whole new low. It brought me inside a luxury car just outside of Monty's Restaurant and Bar. I saw Grant pulling out of Monty's with the Latina Girl in the passenger seat, *in my seat*, and then how long was it, a couple of stop lights? At some point during the short calculated car ride my husband swung into a dark parking lot, set the brake, and then reached for her, this young dark-skinned girl with long black hair that practically poured down her back like fluid, whose last name he didn't bother asking for much less her age.

The question that was hardest to ignore was: *were there others?* Had my husband taken other women to this secret spot, actual adult women who maneuvered and moaned in the front seat of his Audi and then went on their way, back to their apartments, their homes where their husband, maybe even kids awaited them?

Inside me, my nerves snapped and misfired, and I struggled to hold onto my own train of thought, something about when Clara found out about her husband being unfaithful with his employee. But I was only hearing that tearful voice again that I wished I could suffocate into silence. *He stop me. He grab my wrist.* The ink marker I used to write random, important points that came to mind on the board dropped to the ground.

"Hey," the smart-ass started. Apparently, he was concerned that his professor who usually had it all together was suddenly falling apart. He reached down, picked up the marker and handed it to me. The marker was bright green and the ink smelled so strong he joked once in an earlier class when I had my back to him writing with it that he was getting a better high than the weed he'd smoked the night before. "You okay, Professor Nicoli?"

"Thank you," I said, firmly avoiding the question. Then I made much needed eye contact to show that all he'd truly witnessed was a marker slipping out of his professor's hand, nothing more. As a cop, my father faced down danger nightly on the streets. He taught me that keeping composure was comparable to maintaining strength, no matter how weak you felt. Quickly, I caught up to where I'd left off, how Clara had her doubts and hired a private investigator, how David was found with his lover in the same hotel where he married Clara.

"Inside the lobby, Clara waited until she spotted the couple stepping out of the elevator. She tore at the woman's clothing and shouted for all to hear the news that her husband was screwing an employee. David added to his wife's humiliation by pushing her down to the ground and leaving with the woman he came to the hotel with.

To Clara, as she lay in a heap on the floor, he'd made his choice. Their marriage was over. She was escorted out of the hotel by security. Her calmness should've been the first clue to the investigator she'd hired who was outside the hotel filming the blow by blow drama that this so-called love triangle was taking on a new shape. Clara was no longer going to chase after her husband.

As she got into her Mercedes and started the engine, she knew what had to be done. David's daughter from a previous relationship was seated in the passenger seat beside Clara, unaware that she was about to become an unwilling participant in her own father's murder.

David was escorting his lover to her car on the opposite side of the parking lot when Clara sped straight for them. Adding insult to injury, Clara watched as David instinctively protected the woman he loved and pushed her inside the car, taking the brunt impact. Plowing forty miles per hour into her husband's body and hurling him twenty-five feet into the air wasn't enough pain. He needed to hurt more. Like muscle that pulls away from bone, Clara felt the internal separating of her life with the one she'd made with her husband. She felt herself coming apart.

The Mercedes scaled the median and continued to drive over his body, his legs, his arms, his skull crushed beneath the weight of the tires of the luxury car that had once marked their success. As he lay broken, breathing in only shallow bursts, seconds before death, Clara still had enough time to leap out of the car and place blame right where it belonged, saying, "See what you made me do."

The sorority girl smiled down at her desk, a young woman future suitors may not want to cross, then she spoke up.

"Wow, I forgot about that part. That's cold."

I paced back and forth in front of the class to hold their attention.

"How much time do you think it took the jury to deliberate?" I questioned.

Someone in the middle of the lecture hall shouted out, "A couple hours, tops. What's there to deliberate? She's guilty as hell. I mean, c'mon. Her own investigator taped her murdering her husband."

"Try eight hours," I said. "The jury gave her the maximum sentence for sudden passion homicide. Twenty years in prison."

The smart-ass in the front row appeared disgusted.

"Excuse my language, Professor Nicoli, but that's bullshit. She's probably already gone up for parole by now. She'll be out by the end of this decade. Such a double standard. No man would ever just get twenty years if he ran over his wife."

"Maybe," I conceded. "But in the end it was a crime of passion. She loved him. The jury understood what that kind of love can do to a relatively normal person. I think they put themselves in her position. She handled his betrayal the only way she knew how. She killed him."

At the time I was playing devil's advocate, as a professor must. I wasn't defending the husband-killer, but now that I've endured Grant's trial, having to imagine him over and over again unzipping his pants, coercing another female to mouth him, I find a new understanding of the psychological torture in Clara's heart as she sat in the driver's seat and watched him with his lover, why she then hit the gas. Her love for her husband turned dark, turned dangerous.

Through the wall from the bedroom where I'm stuffing a pair of shorts into my suitcase for our trip to the desert, I overhear the muffled sounds of Grant talking on the phone. For a few seconds I contemplate returning to finish the rest of my packing. It could be anyone—Reynolds, Grant's mother or father, even a random telemarketer. Still, after all my husband has put me through these past several months, I'm not so sure he deserves to keep anything more from me. At least this is what I tell myself as I lift the cordless on the nightstand and press *talk*, hearing only a dial tone. He's on his cell which makes me even more curious. I head out into the family room.

Grant clicks off the device without saying goodbye to the other person on the line. The expression on his face tells me I've caught him doing something he'd rather not share with me, and he doesn't. Instead, he goes for a subtle smile.

"Already packed?" my husband, the convicted sex offender, asks.

CHAPTER EIGHT

ACT OF LOVE

Against all better judgment, I lie back on the California King as my husband pushes up my skirt, pulls aside the crotch of my underwear, and I feel him inside me. Too much alcohol has figured into our night and brought us back here to this getaway bungalow in Palm Springs. This is the first time we've tried having sex since before the conviction and sentencing for a crime that has marked my husband as a sexual offender for life. But Grant doesn't know any better. *How could he?* I intentionally show no noticeable signs of resistance. And I am wet for him which must mean I want it, too.

Even my own body seems to be giving in too soon. Time is running out for us. Grant's year long sentence is to start the following Monday after he reports to the Los Angeles Superior Court and gets taken into custody.

He slips two fingers between my lips and crowds his tongue into my mouth. I taste the beer, the bottle after bottle of Dos Equis he nervously drank all through dinner. I get a little taste of his frustration, too. The way he's insisting on kissing me, the way he's pulling out the props, shifting a pillow beneath my hips so that he may move even deeper inside as if doing his best to physically occupy me.

What he wants is for me to open up to him in every way, something I will not do. For a moment he stops, out of breath, his arms braced on either side of my shoulders on the mattress, our bodies locked in the missionary position. His dark eyes battle mine for some sign of emotion. He loves me. I can see that. I've always been able to read his feelings without him having to voice the words. Lightly, he trails his finger down the side of my face with a fragility I'm not expecting.

I could break him, right then, right now, with my cold hard doubts. Instead I wrap my arms around his muscled back in a show of reassurance that there might be hope for the two of us, our marriage. By the way he closes his eyes to kiss me, he seems convinced, or maybe he doesn't want to see that I might just be going through the motions.

Earlier at dinner over sizzling fajitas and a good California Merlot, he kept encouraging me to finish all on my own, he said he knew I'd allow him that close again if "you'd just give it time, Ava." He hadn't called me by my first name since before we were married and it sounded foreign off his tongue, like it came from someone I hardly knew. Whatever it took, he said, if it meant the rest of his life, he'd earn our relationship back.

Even now after the guilty verdict when the truth, Grant's truth at least, no longer matters, he doesn't give up trying to convince me. On the drive here, as we passed a billboard of a bottle of whiskey suspended in a woman's seductive cleavage, Grant had shaken his head, set off by something else.

"Unbelievable...twelve fucking months in prison over some lying little slut. She sat down at my table without my consent. *Without my consent.*"

"Grant," I'd said because I couldn't stand hearing another denial out of him, "we can't keep..." He reached over the console, touching my bare knee as if to stop me from finishing my thought.

"Sorry, V. I'm sorry. Please, forget what I just said."

The heightened image of booze and sex blown up before his eyes triggered his flare up. At trial the bartender had been worthless as a possible witness. He didn't ask for an ID, didn't tell the Latina Girl she couldn't stay in the bar either. He never saw her to begin with. It was busy that late afternoon and he was understaffed. The only middle ground between the Latina Girl's testimony and Grant's was that once at the table she took his glass. Reynolds failed to mention to the jury what a bold move that was, to take Grant's drink. Maybe the thought occurred to him but jurors might've seen that as putting the victim's actions on trial. Teenage girls are coming into their own sexuality. Many of them flirt recklessly, almost instinctively with all males regardless of age. It doesn't mean they deserve to get sexually assaulted.

The rest of her story, after she shared Grant's Stoli on the rocks, where he apparently drove her afterward, what he supposedly coerced her to do in the front seat of his Audi, I don't want to think about. I *can't* think about what my husband may've done with her while he's all over me.

This is the first night of what is supposed to be a nearly week long stay at the Desert Palms Resort. One-on-one counseling, the way Grant and I have always resolved our marital strife—with plenty of sun, poolside cocktails, ditch the shrink. Seeking a third party to act as a mediator in our marriage isn't our style. We are here in the desert, over ninety miles away from home, to repair the fallout of the trial on our relationship. If it wasn't for my husband's brief bout of stupidity, our marriage would be as solid as the walls Grant will be living inside for the next twelve months, our passion for each other nearly as confining. Since we met there has never been any choice but for the two of us to be together.

Only one light is on in the hotel room, the table lamp on Grant's side. I see the first impression other people might have of him—the finely cut suits and a tight, hard body that isn't typical of a middle-age man. Grant takes care of his six-foot-tall physique with punishing workouts at the gym and injects youth back into his body through a daily syringe of human growth hormone prescribed to him by an expensive doctor somewhere out here in the desert. His obvious vanity clearly played into why the jury took less than two hours of deliberation to find him guilty. A man so concerned with his appearance *would* be low enough to seek out the superficial attentions of a teenage girl.

With the flat of my hands, I push at Grant's chest so he will pull out. Our heated breath is overpowered by the smooth mechanical sound of the air cooling and the fluctuating laughter and talk of hotel guests collected around the poolside rock fire pits. Ignoring my gesture for him to stop, my husband keeps a firm hand on my shoulder, spooning me from behind. Then he gathers the hair off my neck and I feel a quick brush of his lips against my skin, a move that always makes me flinch with pleasure.

In an act of real sensitivity he finishes having sex with me with my face pointed toward the wall, as if realizing I can no longer bear to look at him.

The last time we'd made love this way, though without the rush, was in a small whitewashed hotel in the seaport town of Nafplio, Greece. We'd showered off the hot afternoon spent sightseeing along the rocky coast. Then we curled up bare and cool on the bed, Grant stroking me everywhere then focusing on one of his favorite places on me, the sharp curve of my hip. But we hadn't yet had our fill of the beauty of the island. The doors from our balcony opened out to the bright shades of the Aegean Sea. As we lazily dozed on and off for hours, we watched the view gradually darken while Grant eased in hard between my legs, up enough for some drowsy sex.

In the bungalow now, after we both climax, Grant continues to hold me. Even in the cruelest of circumstances he and I have come together. Usually after I'd feel him withdraw, he would say, "I love you, V," and wind up propped with an elbow on his side. The physical disconnect right after sex when the two of us faced each other head on is the most intimate time. We might interlace our fingers and talk about the mundane—share something funny or stressful that happened at work, a terrible movie we'd seen on cable or in the theater. Sometimes our marriage feels so easy like it is a sham, like we are really just friends with benefits, not husband and wife.

But this night proves different. Grant will not play by the established rules. His arms are annoyingly still around me and he will not let go. Silently, it builds, the shame and heartache over all that we've lost bleeds out of me like a gunshot wound, the emotional injury I've sustained by supporting him through the worst kind of criminal charges. My husband has no right to impose anything more on me. Most wives would have taken half of everything and fled the marriage by now. Though, even if I wanted to, there is nothing to take. Our savings are depleted from his lawyer fees and our house is up as collateral for his bail.

Suddenly an alarming force passes through me, a kind of blind rage, the same rage I felt when that blogger accosted me in the women's restroom at the courthouse after the verdict. In the relative dark he must not see how my love for him is beating me up inside, nor does he see the fists I'm making with the sheet.

A shocking picture of him hanging naked from the hotel balcony appears in my mind. The bed sheet works as a noose, his head bent wrong and purpled with blood, the neck snapped at the bone. It would look like suicide. It would look like the last desperate act of a man who could no longer live with himself after what he's done. Pulsing in my bloodstream is the uncontrollable instinct to take matters into my own hands. A genetic remnant passed down from my mother. *"S'agapo,"* my mother had pleaded with him in Greek before firing at him with his own gun.

Grant leans back and hands me a half glass of red wine I must've carried earlier out of the hotel bar.

"You know, V, I'm not…"

"I know."

The wine, when I swallow, tastes bitter, a sign I've already drunk too much. With some effort I balance the glass on the edge of the nightstand on my side.

Grant reaches across me to apparently steady the glass so it won't tip over.

"But you don't seem…"

Everything starts to spin, everything out of place, and it does not stop until I close my eyes and give in to the blackout, as if I haven't any clue my husband won't be here lying next to me by the morning.

CHAPTER NINE

DENIAL

I awaken with the kind of rough hangover that makes me emerge from the down comforter, not stay beneath it. More sobering is the reality that what I'm feeling won't wear off with more sleep or even a handful of aspirin. In just a few short days my husband is being taken from me. Counting down is excruciating. Already the thought of his absence empties me inside. Our hotel room has the same hollowed out quality like things that cannot be undone have happened here.

The room smells like a one night stand, it smells like the rubber condom I insisted my husband wear. Such an intimate separation went beyond the girl. Part of me couldn't bear to feel the warmth of him ejaculating inside me. The other part wanted to rob him of one of the comforts of married sex.

I turn on the side lamp and get up. Grant is no longer in bed, his pillow formed where he lay his head. His car keys, wallet, wedding band, and gold watch are on the nightstand. The bathroom door is open, the light left on, and, typical of my husband, I step on his damp towel. Grant is the type who takes a shower first no matter what. Always the early riser, he must've wanted to swim some free flowing laps in the pool before it becomes obstructed with lounging guests sprawled out on rafts or poking their arms through inner tubes.

On the other side of those drawn heavy drapes are the stirrings of the hotel coming to life in the early morning hour. I pull the blackout drape from the gauzy one used for privacy in the daytime. A blond waiter with the suntan of a local rattles by pushing a room service cart and I realize how badly I want to snatch the silver carafe of coffee. My head pounds from the night before—the bottle of Merlot, the unexpected sex. I have always been a lightweight when it comes to alcohol.

It's been weeks since I've thought clearly. Midway through the trial a dull ache buried itself behind my eyes as I helplessly watched from the first row of the gallery while Grant lost every member on that jury.

Nothing has taken away the pain of knowing Grant's fate, not the affirmation of the guilty verdict, not even the hours spent so far on this vacation to Palm Springs. The Desert Palms Resort is a series of one and two story bungalows that have been refurbished in tacky-chic décor from the early sixties when Frank Sinatra supposedly slept here with Marilyn Monroe. Celebrities continue to make the nearly two hour drive east on the 10 freeway to experience a landscape rich with flat desert scrub and lush sloping golf courses. There is a certain anonymity amongst the wealthy retirees with leather skin, the pale Canadian tourists, and resort hotels with rounds of faceless guests.

The bathroom has a long narrow shower with glass doors big enough to shut in a party of two, and in a trendy hotel like this it probably has accommodated far more naked bodies at a time. I run the warm water but then turn it off. My feet feel too unsteady to withstand a shower just yet. There are things I know for certain and gaps in time from the night before that I can't fill no matter how hard I try to remember. I can't recall much of dinner or what suggestive remark or gesture led us back to the room.

At the sink I expose the underside of my wrists and run cold water from the tap. Through the mirror I see the wear from the trial at the corners of my eyes, tiny scratch-like wrinkles that only recently surfaced. Grant jokes I have found the fountain of youth in the form of my lashes that are so unnaturally long they look as if I use a prescription solution to grow them. But I wonder if the next year that my husband will spend in prison and the subsequent years once he's out having to register as a sex offender won't age me well beyond my thirty-nine years.

On the counter next to the hotel room hair dryer rests the monogrammed shaving bag, slightly unzipped, that I'd bought him as a stocking stuffer one Christmas. I'd surprised him with a ski trip to Tahoe too, but we never hit the slopes. We stayed in bed only getting up sashed in the bathrobes that came with the room to retrieve what extravagant, high caloric meals we'd ordered off the room service menu—fettuccini alfredo, the chef's specialty of Pacific cod in a white wine and capers sauce. Later at home, Grant complained in the midst of late night stomach crunches that he'd gained three whole pounds, but that he'd do a million more crunches if it meant experiencing me naked for seventy-two hours straight again.

He and I were so much happier then in that hotel room, than we are in this one. I remember the reason I'm up so early isn't necessarily alcohol driven. I have an appointment for a deep tissue massage at The Healing Joint Spa downtown. I search through my suitcase for the gray sweatshirt I packed, a pair of shorts, and some flip-flops.

On my way to the car I decide not to look for Grant. The pool is in the opposite direction and I tell myself there isn't enough time. I'm not ready to face him, to crouch down at the pool's edge and wait as he glides up to the surface for a kiss. I'm not ready to taste the chlorine on his lips while he gives off that recently fucked glow. We've made love, he'll think to himself, therefore our relationship is back on track. The leverage I've always maintained in my marriage is my husband's inability to predict what my next move will be.

◆

THE MASSAGE LASTS A full hour. Scented candles, soft classical music, a man's warm strong hands spreading out all over my body. The set-up is like the obvious foreplay that Grant and I passed on the night before. I'm sure he would've slowed down if I'd asked, but I was afraid I might not go through with it, that much I remember.

He has probably padded dry with a hotel beach towel, cinched it at the waist, and is on his way back to the room by now or he's thrown on a shirt and is kicking back at the hotel restaurant with some fresh fruit and yogurt. There was no need for me to leave a note since the massage was Grant's idea. My cell phone is in my purse in the ladies locker room if he tries to call. Grant has complained that I've inexplicably changed my number again. But it is better if he thinks it's just me being neurotic over wrong numbers and too many telemarketers.

Somehow Martin had tracked it down. As a Superior Court judge, he is a man with too many connections he abuses, and an ego no amount of beautiful women can quell. He is a man who forgets nothing and I owe him for, among other things, removing the blogger that afternoon from the courthouse. Already he has burned through a scant marriage and two engagements since I broke it off with him after I met Grant.

There hadn't been much to break off. A couple of casual dates, and yet Martin couldn't let go of the fact that I'd ended our relationship. After he sentenced Miguel, a nineteen-year-old client to the maximum five years on a first time drug offense, I knew I had to stop showing my face in Judge Durham's courtroom. When a full time lectureship opened up at a state university in the Valley, I applied for the position and got it. This upcoming semester I'll be teaching everything from California law to capital murder to my criminal justice undergraduates.

In order to be together, Grant had to leave far more. He left a wealthy blonde bride and his share of the multimillion dollar beachfront home in Laguna Niguel they'd furnished together. At times resentment has to hit whenever he pulls into the drive of our small two bedroom home in Studio City or he and I disagree about something. There must be moments when he questions if he's done the right thing by rushing into a second marriage with a public defender turned university lecturer.

The masseuse continues working on a particularly stubborn muscle in my shoulder, strained as if I'd slept wrong or physically lifted something too heavy.

"Would you like me to stop?" he asks.

"No," I say. Lying face down on the massage table, my head fitted in that cut out space so my back is perfectly aligned, I get a close-up view of the man's shoes. They're expensive Italian loafers, not tennis shoes, the common footwear for a masseuse.

"I must've pulled it yesterday while swimming."

A lie comes out before I can think of the truth. My black one piece is buried at the bottom of my suitcase, completely dry.

◆

LATER AT THE STARBUCKS downtown, as I feed coins into the machine for *The Desert Sun* newspaper, I notice two of my nails are snapped to the pinks. An ugly bruise is surfacing on the inside of my left forearm. If someone saw my injuries it might appear that I'd been in some kind of heated struggle.

I drop the sleeve of my sweatshirt. The caffeine is doing its number on my hangover because with every sip the fatigue lessens and clarity is coming back to me. This is when I decide to turn on my phone.

There are no messages on my voice mail from Grant, just one from my father. "Call me, *Kitsoli*," he says. The affection in his voice can't hide the concern. He leaves out the reason why I need to call him back. He was at closing arguments, he heard the verdict, the sentencing, and knows his son-in-law is on borrowed time.

Winter mornings are cool in the desert, blue cloudless skies, a comfortable seventy degrees. People are taking full advantage sitting at the tables outside the coffee place. Two men, one dressed for an office job, the other in workout gear, huddle close sharing the paper. An older woman in sunglasses chats away on a cell phone, a bored Irish Setter heeling at her side. Nothing seems to be weighing on them, no emotional baggage, no worry about an uncertain future, no underage minority girl with heartbreaking English. The two men are clearly lovers. The one in a shirt and tie pats his partner's thigh from under the table. They share a whisper, something that makes them both smile.

With my Venti black coffee, my cell phone now turned off again, I take a seat at a free table. I snap up the front page of the paper and pretend that what my husband and I need, even with the clock nearly up on Grant's freedom, are a couple more hours spent apart.

CHAPTER TEN

ABANDONMENT

Some kind of lively conference of women who don't need men is happening in the hotel bar. The loud talk and laughter draws me in when I should be checking on my husband. It's past three in the afternoon, well past my massage appointment, and he has yet to try my cell. The heavy sweatshirt I put on this morning doesn't look right in a room full of bikinis with see-through cover-ups and dresses with high slits.

I like the anonymity, the way I've practically disappeared. Men have always given me too much attention, in restaurants, in courtrooms, even a groom at his own wedding reception.

Tight golden legs or fleshy thighs, this is not a self-conscious crowd. The women might be trying to hook up with each other because it appears they've driven most of the opposite sex out of the room. For all I know the Dinah Shore golf tournament might be going on.

I haven't followed much of anything lately except Grant's trial. He made sure of my commitment to his court proceedings by finding the money to buy me time off from teaching. Oftentimes, his generosity has a selfish, edge like this trip. No spontaneous Christmas present, this trip *was* planned by my husband—minutes before Reynolds called that the verdict was in—as a consolation prize or a parting gift, definitely a manipulation. *Please don't divorce me while I'm in prison.*

The bar counter where I'm seated sipping ice water exposes a perfect view of the pool and white canvas cabanas. For a good half hour I've watched for my husband when I know he isn't out there. By now Grant will be back in our room taking an afternoon nap as he typically does after a workout or when we're on vacation.

Most likely he is on the phone settling last minute details before his incarceration. These kind of hushed calls are handled on his way into another room because he doesn't want to upset me more, which, of course, only reinforces the fact he continues to keep things from me.

His investment banking position at a known firm in Century City was in jeopardy long before the allegations. If the economy continues to slowly stabilize he is assured an office to come back to but verbal reassurances aren't the same as the only kind that matters, a legal iron clad promise of employment I offered to draft up for his boss to sign. Grant had turned it down, irritably saying on occasion I should try trusting someone's word.

The physical effects of last night's alcohol have burned off and it's time for a cool stiff one, maybe a Long Island Iced Tea. A fresh young bartender with long bangs has just come on shift and I motion to him. He winks awkwardly, new to the job. Hotel policy probably calls for him to address every woman as "Miss" even if she's a quaking eighty-year-old with dentures.

In the far corner, a Mexican man is positioned with an eye on everything, including me. Undercover hotel security? He's hardly subtle, at a table alone sucking on a soft drink. The practical, unstylish button down shirt gives him away and the kind of face even his wife might lose in a busy Target store where they must shop on the weekends for everything from a new garden hose to bananas.

Carl, the bartender, it says so on his badge, comes over with a full glass of Merlot.

Showing up with my favorite drink is a condemnation from the night before and I think twice about the mixed drink I'm about to order. Grant and I must've been good drunk tippers.

"Is your husband joining you?" The question sounds doubtful, cocky out of his mouth like I might be more of a sexual possibility than a customer.

I shake my head.

"He's back in the room."

Immediately it hits me, that this bartender witnessed something get out of hand between me and my husband. Yesterday, after Grant's outburst in the car about the Latina Girl, he and I agreed not to talk about the trial, though a conversation fueled by alcohol was the fastest way of putting our truce to the test.

"Too much liquor draws out stupid disagreements about the cap on the toothpaste," I say. Or that devastating Stoli on the rocks a married man shared with a teenage girl in a populated bar. None of this wreckage would be happening if Grant had been smart enough to see that girl for what she was.

Carl studies me, my make-up free face, the sweatshirt, the look of a woman who's recovering from a hangover.

"Toothpaste, huh?"

"Yeah," I answer. "Toothpaste."

"You two went at it pretty good, but not for long."

I swivel off the stool. That part is right. Our arguments never last more than a flurry of fighting words before we cool off in separate corners of the house. But we aren't at home. We're cramped together in a hotel room which changes things, *changes us*. With the two of us under so much stress lately, speculating each other's limits might be a mistake.

As a lawyer I am accustomed to speaking convincingly. "It was nothing."

The bartender looks as if he believes me.

I decide to pass on the drink.

Our hotel room is two buildings away in the back bordering the dense hedge that separates the property from busy Palm Canyon Road, the two lane route that leads directly out of the city to the 10 freeway. Chandeliers, with black twisted wrought iron and dark ruby colored stones, dangle from the ceiling every couple of feet. The wallpaper is maroon, the carpet a new form of black shag. The lobby and hallways of this hotel have the decorative flair of a bordello on the outskirts of Vegas.

Last night, down the hallway, a woman could be heard screaming out from behind one of these closed doors. Her voice sounded too loud, too practiced, an erotic put on for show not necessarily pleasure. For a moment Grant and I stopped to listen like auditory voyeurs. Her screams turned into a pretty convincing plea. She needed to get fucked harder.

Grant cocked his head to the side the way he always does when he's not being serious.

"That's hot."

I tried not to smile.

"No, that's a hooker."

I grabbed Grant's arm to pull him closer.

I had.

Me.

The one of us who tore the other away, the one who as it turned out made the first move. There was my body fitted up against his though I stopped short of kissing him.

His breath mingled with mine. He knew better than to move any closer, break whatever connection he and I were actually making. I still hated what he'd done to us to start this out with something as personal as a kiss. For the night, I would play the whore with the lungs on the other side of that wall, not his wife.

Grant understood. He left me standing there, listening to the screamer while he grabbed the wine I'd left on the table in the bar. He didn't want to risk me losing my buzz, gaining cold hard perspective.

The Do Not Disturb card Grant had tagged last night onto the knob is missing from our door. Housekeeping has been by to exchange our waste with bleached white bath towels, wrapped soaps, and mini luxurious lotions and shampoo. Inside the room the dread overwhelms me, the meticulous order of my things coupled with Grant's. Our suitcases side by side on the fold-out racks in the closet.

The only things housekeeping haven't touched are Grant's gold watch, car keys, wallet, and wedding band that are still on the nightstand. No longer do they appear left behind for a swim or some other excursion on the hotel grounds. I know what they would look like to the police, if I were to call them. They would see the items as physical evidence of a person who is now missing.

CHAPTER ELEVEN

LUST

Grant and I met at his wedding to his first wife Margaret. The formality of her name already clued me in to the fact that she came from old Orange County money, from conservative parents who prided themselves on giving their children allowances and chores so they could talk at dinner parties about how *their* children knew the price of the silver spoon they were eating from. Weekends were spent at a second home overlooking the golf course of a private country club in the resort town of Lake Arrowhead.

I wasn't being critical of her as I was envious. My father, before the shooting, worked a second job as a security guard to try and keep up with my mother's confusing spending sprees. She'd order a new leather sofa and matching love seat that didn't even fit in our cramped family room or a second double door refrigerator she placed in the garage to store the extra gallons of milk and orange juice that always expired before we could drink them. Her obsession for material things was manageable until she flipped that fixation on to her husband and what he was doing whenever he was away from her.

All those hours he spent working off her debt, she repaid with nonstop calls to his jobs. She'd cry inconsolably, cursing at him for being a no-good-son-of-a-bitch cheater. Sometimes he'd leave work early, but when her fits became too frequent, he secretly bought me a throwaway phone and packed it with minutes. At twelve I was old enough to call him if one of her tirades got too out of hand and I was afraid she might harm herself. Back then, neither of us realized the person she was planning on hurting was him.

Martin insisted I come with him as his date to the reception held at a five star ocean front hotel in Laguna Nigel, an entire beach town that seemed to be perched on a cliff.

I still wasn't sure what to make of him.

After he let my client charged with shoplifting a flatscreen TV go with a hearty warning, not even probation, he sent his secretary after me the way a rock star would his manager pimp. "Judge Durham wants to see you in his chambers," she'd said. When I walked into his office a Greek feast awaited me—Souvlaki,

Spanokopita, and grape leaves marinated and stuffed. It was all very flattering but I also felt set up, instantly on edge. Since then we'd gone out to dinner a couple of times with me making excuses at my front door about briefs I needed to write as I slowly reached for my house key and slipped out of another long goodnight kiss. Soon I'd either have to break up with him or let him in, in every way.

Maybe it was his money. It was hard to trust a man who drove the legal limit in a white Volvo sedan during the work week and sped through red lights on the weekends in a black Porsche Carrera. Judge Martin Durham always seemed to be putting on an act like attending the wedding of a woman he hadn't seen in literally decades. Margaret and Martin had gone to the same private high school in Newport Beach, they had the same circle of friends. Although a perfect match for each other, Martin didn't seem to think so. "Not my type," he said, evasively when I asked. "Turned out she's too much like me."

If I was curious whether Martin was the kind of guy who ended romantic relationships amicably, at the reception I noticed he approached her groom, not her. A big band was playing classic love standards and Margaret was holding court clear across the other side of the banquet hall. She was showing off her second white dress of the evening, a tighter silk cocktail dress, with a steady sway of her hips that was out of sync with the music. She couldn't do much moving balanced on such spiked toothpick stilettos.

Martin would later take great pains to remind me, his decision to sidestep the bride and instead have the two of us speak with her groom ruined our relationship and in time I would feel the hurt. I would feel the same helpless kind of hurt he felt when he watched Grant and I interact for that first time. Whenever Martin had the chance he opened old wounds with a closed case file *The State of California Vs. Iris Nicoli*. "What kind of daughter watches her own father get shot in the back? You were twelve," he'd say. "Couldn't you've done something? Well, I guess you did by just standing there. I wonder how you live with yourself every time Dad wheels toward you and you bend down to give him a great big hug."

Martin was wrong about how that night happened between my mother and father, but he was right about one thing. He'd made the irreversible mistake of introducing me to Margaret's new husband. Grant stared at me with that knowledge that passes between two people who are attracted enough to become lovers without saying a word to each other. As a criminal justice professor, I know the stats. I've done the research. Instant passion for a total stranger is overwhelming and typically a safety mechanism kicks in. A compelling case of morality rescues one from the other. After all, there are more of us in committed relationships than there are those who are single.

Immediately, Grant turned his attention on Martin.

"How long have you known Margaret?"

It was a polite question, appropriate enough except for the fact he left out the wife part. A new groom might've wanted to try out the word since he'd just made a big show of saying their vows to a captive audience.

Somehow during the course of a conversation that lasted less than five minutes, Grant got me to give him the name of the gym I sometimes frequented after work. It was all the information he'd need should he want to reassure a second meeting. And he wasn't so sure he wanted to ever see me again. "I could've killed you," Grant said in my bed shortly after he'd left Margaret. "Wrung that slender neck of yours feeling your life leak out of all my ten fingers. You turned my world upside fucking down then left with another man."

This is the part I always fuzzily relay to Grant, how the rest of the night with Martin played out.

On our way to Martin's black Porsche, Martin was quiet, thinking.

The ocean air smelled unclean and below us the water we couldn't see sounded rough.

"You like him," Martin finally said.

"I like that we left before they cut the cake," I added quickly, trying to lighten up his dark mood. "I don't think I can stand seeing another couple smearing frosting over each other's faces. That's an obnoxious, not to mention messy tradition."

Martin mumbled something that I couldn't make out as he opened the car door for me and strangely waited until I got in before he pulled my safety belt on, locking me in place.

Inside the car, Martin turned on the engine, adjusted the rear view mirror, then shook his head. He killed the engine. The way he suddenly looked at me nearly made me get out of the car. Part of me was afraid he was about to punch me in the face, bloody my nose or blacken my eyes. I could've jumped out of the car but what would I have been running from? A cold stare? A man who had every reason to be irritated at his date?

A jazzy sounding Bryan Ferry from the eighties when he was a part of Roxy Music surrounded us courtesy of his car's high tech sound system. The song seemed to calm Martin and he reached across me and lowered my seat back, his eyes focused on the hem of my short black dress that had ridden up. His head was weighted on my lap, and he was breathing hard like he was sick with something.

I stroked his hair because it wasn't that I didn't like him. It was just that he already was feeling too much for me, and I doubted if I'd ever be able to catch up.

An older couple passed by the car while Martin slid my black thong completely off, but I doubted they could see in. The windows were so darkly tinted that he would be ticketed if he was anybody but a high ranking judge. I slipped my hand behind his neck and encouraged him to taste me for what would be the first and last time.

Not unlike a man who has a woman kneel before him and take him deep into her throat, then afterward she looks up at him in the hopes that this sex act has somehow changed things, brought them closer. But sometimes issues of power and submission have little to do with it. Sometimes words will only make things worse and sex where one is receiving gratification over the other is the only way out of a situation that has gone too far.

CHAPTER TWELVE

PANIC

Most people when faced with a spouse who has disappeared would call the police. And I know I am making myself look suspicious by not doing so. But if I go to the cops, Grant's bond will be revoked. I'll lose more than just my husband—I'll lose the house we live in that we put up for the bond. I am relying on everything inside our home, the domestic order of our married life, to get through his sentence because it's my sentence, too. For the year my husband will be serving out his time, I plan on keeping his toothbrush in the steel holder alongside mine, keeping his suits hanging in their dry cleaning wrap on his side of the walk-in closet, brewing the same Italian Roast he and I drink every morning before heading off to work.

Like a death, my husband's personal things and maintaining our daily rituals will be all I have left of him.

I'll also lose a lot of time being questioned. The drill would start off friendly enough inside our hotel room while one of the two investigators glanced around taking a cursory inventory of things, deciding if there was evidence that an altercation happened here. They might even waste more time taking me to the station and strapping me to a lie detector machine. The spouse is always the prime suspect and given the recent trial, ruling me out will take more time than I have to find him.

On the off chance I'm wrong that Grant is gone, I check his wallet. Inside the fold are a couple of credit cards, his California driver's license. Nobody ever takes a good photo at the DMV except for my husband who looks amused like someone has just told him a dirty joke. Even his passport photo is centered and in proportion unlike mine, which is too close up and shows I didn't get enough sleep the night before. He had to surrender it to the court months back as part of the request to be out on bail.

There are a couple of crisp business cards, colleagues from work, professionals with monied titles he must've met at expensive lunches, nothing stands out. No telling phone number written down in pen on the back.

In an inside hidden slit of his wallet is a picture of me taken at my father's last birthday celebration. I am posed in front of the cake, a big wax 7 and 0 candle planted in the chocolate frosting like I am the senior citizen. My smile is real, meant for my husband, for the afternoon he and I shared with my father. It's a corny pose, one that

I'd forgotten Grant had even caught on camera let alone kept it in his wallet. Grant and I haven't laughed together in months.

As for cash, he only had a few hundred on him. My breath sounds shallow in the quiet of our bungalow. How would I be able to find him if everything I could track him down with is not on him but instead baiting me right here in our hotel room? It is what I don't see that gives me pause, the most important thing Grant never leaves behind, and I grab my cell and press down on the first key that is programmed for his number.

A faint buzzing instantly snuffs out all hope that I'm wrong about my husband intentionally leaving me. Stashed in his suitcase, beneath a pair of jeans is his phone. My fourth call of the day has not been picked up. My fingers scan and scan, the information all blurry. His contact numbers are about as helpful as the business cards in his wallet. The only thing that seems out of place is a call he took the day before from Margaret. Why would his ex-wife be calling? Was she offering her support or rubbing it in?

It is hard to tell with Margaret because even though she's moved on with a new husband, our affair had embarrassed her, made her a divorcée, even though she'd technically had her marriage to Grant annulled.

I rifle through his entire suitcase, the pouch where he keeps his dress socks folded, not knotted. I check the inside pockets of his jeans that still smell of dryer sheets and come up with nothing.

The day before, shortly after we checked in, Grant and I headed to a well-lit casino downtown, a colorful one built for tourists, not local down-on-their-luck gamblers. It's where we first started drinking. It's where one goes to lose complete track of time. Blinking lights, noise, and cheap alcohol. Grant and I were together without actually being together. I'd sat on a stool playing the same quarter slot machine while Grant was at a live game table, playing blackjack.

At some point Grant had come by, slipped two C-notes in my machine.

"I forgot to pack a couple toiletries," he'd said. "Be right back."

Among the items he must've purchased was a box of condoms, which he readily had on him last night. His aftershave, when he bent down to kiss my cheek, was more powerful than the smoke, the pungent deodorizers used to camouflage the reek of humanity, the hot rush of high rollers and those lowly losers breaking out in a sweat.

I realize now that Grant was buying time with those two hundred dollar bills, and I check the business cards in his wallet again. His growth hormone doctor has his practice out here in the desert. Knowing Grant, no matter how fleeting the effects might be, he would get one last shot of youth before prison aged him.

The doctor's professional medical specialty startles me. Dr. Anthony Maroni, Oncologist. The address is a suite in Palm Desert. For some reason I expect hormone replacement therapy to be tied to a plastic surgeon, a breast and face man with an overexposed woman on a billboard advertising his remarkable services on the side of the freeway. Not a man who treats the dying, nobly improving the quality of life for AIDS and cancer patients.

Impulsively, I dial his number unsure of what I'll say. The clock on the nightstand reads 4:36 p.m. Doctors rarely stay late. My questions might have to wait until the morning.

After two rings a tired female receptionist picks up.

"Yes, I'm sorry to be calling so late." My voice turns polite and businesslike, impressive, I think, for a woman who has no clue where to find her convicted felon of a husband. "I'm Mr. Grant Jacobson's assistant and I'd like to confirm his appointment for tomorrow morning at nine thirty."

Over the line, paper rustles, the sound of confusion, the pages of an appointment book being flipped back and forth. I wonder why appointments aren't logged more conveniently on the computer unless there is a protocol of separating superficial injectable patients from the doctor's more legitimate practice.

"There must be a mistake," the female assistant says pleasantly. "He was in to see the doctor yesterday at three."

Grant lied to me.

I hang up the phone. I will have to wait until the morning to find out if he went in for more than a treatment. Maybe the doctor had become a friend of

some kind, someone my husband could confide in. Grant
is charming that way even though the truth is he'd much
rather be alone. People always want to become a part of
his world which is why there is the possibility he is telling
the truth about the girl. It has crossed my mind more
than once that Martin is somehow involved, that he paid
her to test Grant's fidelity and to Martin's amusement,
Grant failed. Throughout the trial Martin made a point
of showing up in the hall to check on me as if he had
someone giving him blow by blow commentary of
Grant's proceedings.

Maybe the girl had been picked up for shoplifting
and Judge Durham offered her a below the belt way
to expunge her record. It came out in the trial that her
parents are here illegally. Martin could've placed some
calls and helped fast track them to American citizenry.
But then the practical professor side of me tells me not
to turn into that unhinged wife desperate to cling to
something, no matter how flimsy, that would excuse her
husband for being unfaithful.

Before I changed my number, Martin called off
and on until I simply stopped picking up. Eventually I
assumed he'd give up. He is seeing the new one, that
red headed court reporter with the ivory typing fingers
poised for action. But no woman ever knows how to
hold his interest for long except for me. I held it because I
broke it off with him and he can't tolerate rejection. Had
I angered him enough to put my husband behind bars?
Would Martin really go that far?

I don't want to think about how he'll reach out to me now that Grant will be locked away for the next twelve months.

Physically I'm not doing well. My stomach seizes in cramps that come and go because I haven't eaten all day. A floating sensation overcomes me and my wrists feel unattached to my hands. I'm exhausted. I look down at the bruise that has darkened during the last few hours. Black grit is under a nail I hadn't noticed before.

Inside the bathroom I unwrap a fresh bar of soap and stand beneath the near burning water because I need to feel something. I can hear what the cops would say if they knew. *She placed one phone call. Just one. No doubt for show. Then she took a nice hot shower and ordered a hamburger and fries from room service. That's one cold bitch.*

I don't know how to explain why my appetite is back. I do order dinner, actually I order for two because there is no need to arouse the hotel staff's curiosity. After all Grant's Audi is taking up space in the guest parking lot. Before the waiter knocks with the tray of food, I take Grant's personal effects and hide them in a drawer.

◆

IN THE MIDDLE OF the night my cell phone rings. I sit up, groggy because I've been sleeping hard for hours. The TV is on, an old episode of *Law and Order*. My half-eaten room service meal from last night is on the bed beside me. Circumstantial evidence for the cops. *She actually finished off the fries. An innocent wife would be too upset to eat.* The number on the screen shows it's an unknown call.

"Hello," I say once, twice. It doesn't seem to matter to the person on the other end which prompts me to get out of bed and onto my feet. There is the slightest chance it's my husband checking up on me. He's afraid to speak because he doesn't want me shouting at him, furious that he sought time to himself when ironically time to himself is all he'll have in the coming year.

In the background I hear something I can't quite place, something muffled like a hand smothering noise.

If it is Grant, he knows not to scare me this way. This isn't the man I married.

I don't want to give this person the satisfaction of my fear so I, too, say nothing, a silent game of chicken.

The line goes dead.

I try calling back but it just rings and rings. For safe measure I check the lock on the slider that leads out to the balcony. The hefty bolt is secure on the hotel's front door but it wouldn't take much for someone to come in through the slider, seconds really to break the glass. If I made it to the phone to dial hotel security the fat Target-shopper from the bar would take too long to hustle down to my rescue. Besides I doubt he's armed with anything more lethal than pepper spray, maybe a taser.

I do my best to lay back down to bed but the caller got his way because I am wide awake now.

◆

TECHNICALLY, TWENTY-FOUR HOURS HAVE passed since I've last seen my husband. It's not too late for me to call the police. Typically this is the right time to call them, an entire day of me searching and waiting over, when they might actually start taking what I say seriously. Would it really be so hard to rule me out as a suspect or am I afraid of the other direction they may go? Grant has four days left before he is to turn himself in to a courtroom in downtown LA, his arms shackled behind his back by an expressionless bailiff I'll probably recognize by name. Some might even call Grant a fugitive now. Border security from Canada to Mexico might be notified, shown his picture to be on the lookout.

My outfit is casual, a skirt, fitted T-shirt and strappy sandals because it's important for me to keep up the appearance of a tourist, something I stopped being the moment my travel companion disappeared. Most of the other meal I ordered the night before gets flushed in nauseating chunks down the toilet. From a cop show on cable I've now switched to the local morning news. It's going to be a balmy eighty degrees before the night plummets down to the low forties, whiplash weather.

So far the details of Grant's trial and sentencing aren't replaying in a loop on the local desert morning news shows. No one fitting his description has been arrested in the area either, but if it comes out he is missing that will make him a headlining fugitive. Instantly he'll be national news, a celebrity of sorts, trailed by police instead of paparazzi similar to the Barefoot Bandit or cosmetics heir Andrew Luster.

Like any other hotel guest I leave the tray and plates out on the floor in front of my room. Housekeeping can't keep traipsing through here so I tidy up in the bungalow which doesn't take long considering I only slept on my side of the bed.

On my way out of the room I hang the Do Not Disturb sign on the knob to make it seem like Grant is sleeping in.

The lobby is charged with activity—employees on friendly autopilot in dark vests check in new guests and wish the ones leaving a safe trip home. It's a Thursday, a day before things really get crazy here with the weekenders. A fresh stack of newspapers is next to the silver carafes of decaf and regular coffee and half-and-half on the counter. I pour myself some straight black coffee in a paper to-go cup. The smell of eggs overwhelms the air.

Parking attendants dart with claim checks to fetch cars. Grant and I aren't cheap, though neither one of us has the patience to wait even if we're on vacation. I head out to the self-parking lot.

Grant's Audi is in the same spot where I left it the day before except with a brand new white Jaguar parked next to it. I click off the alarm and get inside Grant's car. The interior is immaculate, strokes of polished mahogany on the steering wheel and along the dash. His presence is still felt in the lingering scent of his aftershave and for a moment I take him in, I breathe him. A part of me regrets last night's shower, rinsing his touch off my body when that's all I had left. How far I've come from only being able to picture him in this car with her, the Latina Girl. Because he's disappeared, could I actually be believing more in his innocence or have I finally found a way to temporarily purge that scene with the two of them from my mind?

Grant does not like to play games. There *is* a logical reason why he's not here. I just have to figure it out. As the engine warms I comb through the interior of his car. I pull down the visor, check the inside door, lift up the console, finding nothing inside but a small silver leaden flashlight for emergencies. I run my hand under his driver's seat and touch on something. It's a parking stub for a place somewhere downtown in LA nowhere near his work or mine. It could be old and irrelevant because the time stamp is smudged, yet it's all I have, that and a phone call Grant took the day before from his ex-wife.

The rear view mirror is still fixed from when I drove the car to my massage appointment which seems so long ago now. My cell goes off and while I should get it, this time I force myself not to pick up. After last night I do not want anyone using scare tactics to stop me from getting the answers I need.

◆

DR. MARONI'S OFFICE IS on the third floor of an all glass medical building in Palm Desert, a city that is caught in mid-sprawl with new restaurants and condominium complexes suddenly rising up blocks away from each other on a stretch of desert dust. It is a growing community that feels a little architecturally confused, not sure if it's building up for retired couples locked away in pricey gated housing or for young singles and families in one story homes with flat rooftops and a front yard for kids to play in. Sitting off from the freeway is an Indian casino made of stucco that resembles an old style insane asylum.

From a good couple hundred yards away, I sit and wait in Grant's car. There is no chance I'll miss Maroni pulling in. My view is perfect. Toward the elevators are the reserved spaces for the doctors. Several sips of my coffee later, a black Lexus sedan pulls into Dr. Maroni's space.

He is tall, not exactly attractive with a thick neck that makes his balding head appear smaller than it probably is like things do in the side mirror of a car. His skin is a strange shade of tan, too even for sunlight or the ultraviolet rays of a tanning salon. Grant told me about a new injectable, hot to the market that tans a person from the inside, no sun required. Dr. Maroni took up the side practice of testosterone, steroids and new skin procedures to test them out for himself.

I get out of the car and give the doctor plenty of space so that he doesn't sense me coming and turn to see who is behind him. He walks steadily, nearly too fast for me to catch up, and I hope he isn't taking the stairs that are directly next to the pair of elevators.

He stops in time and pushes the elevator button, lighting it up. When the elevator doors open I slip inside with him, a friendly smile exchanged between us. A wet coffee stain is on his cream colored shirt. His eyes are a watery blue. Contacts. Nothing about this man, I realize, is actually real.

"Excuse me," I say. "My husband is a patient of yours, "Grant Jacobsen."

He holds up a soft hand with an impressively sized ruby ring squeezing the life out of his pinkie finger.

"I don't give out information on my patients, Mrs. Jacobsen, no matter the relationship."

His response is predictable. I've cross-examined my share of medical experts and typically they're all arrogant and smug. But no doctor is immune to the government entity that will bring them down. Even if they're clean, threatening to report them to the state medical board is a doctor's Achilles heel.

"I need to know if all he came in for yesterday was a testosterone shot."

The elevator bobs to a stop.

My finger is already holding down the closed button, sounding the buzzer.

"I'd hate to have to report your practices to the California Medical Board," I continue. "Something tells me pumping patients like my healthy husband with testosterone and steroids isn't part of an oncologist's job."

Dr. Maroni has taken the hit and it shows on his face. For years he has probably gotten away with his side practice, one of the desert's best kept secrets. The shock wears off and his expression relaxes some. He knows my price.

"Seconal," Dr. Maroni says. "Check the pharmacy on Highway 111 in Rancho Mirage. That's where most of my patients get their prescriptions filled."

Before I ask why my husband who never took more than an aspirin would want something so strong, Dr. Maroni has pushed the button to open the elevator doors. Understandably he can't get away from me fast enough. The day has barely begun and the back of his business shirt is already wrinkled like someone has grabbed him and roughed him up from behind.

◆

THE PHARMACY IS STASHED away in an older looking strip mall next to Happy Hands nail salon and a big chain grocery store. With every step, Dr. Maroni's reputation gets sketchier and sketchier. The shelves are barely stocked, one or two boxes of muscle rub deep. A layer of dust has collected on the candy bars on display in front of the register. Customers who come in and out of this place aren't here to pick up a snack.

No respected doctor would send his patients here. It has the skeletal markings of a front, that if the DEA barged in, has a drill in place to flush the drugs fast.

A young chemist with no degree is probably at work in the back, cooking up the vials Dr. Maroni prescribes to his cash only patients with face lifts and deep pockets who will pay through the nose not to look their age. The real patients with the real diseases whose visits are billed to their insurance company must be routed to legitimate pharmacies. The girl behind the counter who might be in her early twenties is wearing a white lab coat that looks like a costume, like it should come with a toy stethoscope.

After I tell her our last name, she goes to a plastic tub with a system of rows, one tiny white bag after the other. Grant couldn't have possibly gone through with it and picked up the prescription. There were no pills in his suitcase, in his shaving kit or in his car.

The girl comes back with her arms outstretched in a cute shrug.

"Sorry. He must've picked them up yesterday."

Her words are deadening, and I turn quickly because I won't let a stranger in a coat two sizes too big see my pain.

He's planned it all out and left me, his own wife, like a loose end. The Seconal explains the headache that took all day to get over. He must've used it to drug me the night before, sunk a couple tiny pills in my wine glass when he brought it back from the restaurant, right before he and I had sex. But why would he bother? I'd drunk too much wine anyway and was going to sleep. Why would he need me knocked out cold?

I picture him in a Motel 6 laid out, fully dressed, on a floral printed bedspread, thin and quilted. Or he could've made prior arrangements for a car and drove, just drove, maybe taking a side road until there was nothing but sagebrush and sand dunes. He parked the rental, turned off the engine, rolled up the windows and waited for the internal shock of his organs shutting down in all the wrong order. Suicide by pills is not a slow peaceful sleep like so many people like to think. It's real minutes of real agony, it's an intolerable pain, a poisoning of the bloodstream.

Grant isn't the type to leave a suicide note behind. He would find it too confessional, too weak. My husband is the type to see to it that not even his body will be found.

CHAPTER THIRTEEN

CONTROL

I am not so much fleeing the scene as I am heading back toward my life with Grant, looking for answers. After all, there is no actual body. Not to mention there is too much ground to cover here in the desert. Calling cheap motels in the area and driving out of the city along nowhere roads would've been one way of searching for him. If I was a wife, clueless to her husband's whereabouts, that's exactly what I'd do. If I were her, this is about the time I might also notify the police, call Reynolds, my father, confiding in anyone I could about the bottle of Seconal.

But I am not that kind of wife. I also have more to go on than the assumption my husband has killed himself.

Like if Grant had been planning to swallow all those pills and take his own life, why not do it somewhere familiar like his own car? It was parked, within a short walking distance of our room, in the guest parking lot of the hotel. This elaborate scheme where he takes me along for part of the ride and leaves me at a dead end doesn't make any sense. The looming thought of prison could be distorting his judgment because Grant would not purposely set out to hurt me.

Thousands of giant white windmills with elongated blades border the 10 freeway, a sign you are either entering or leaving Palm Springs. They churn up enough natural energy to light up the city as well as some nearby suburbs. Some people call these electrical powerhouses an eye sore, a blight to the bland beauty of the desert, while others have captured them as a striking landmark. Photos of the windmills spin on postcard racks along with pictures of the Spruce Goose and the bronze statue of the late beloved mayor, Sonny Bono, that sits for all to pose with in front of a fountain downtown.

I have two leads—one obviously more credible than the other. Margaret's gallery is located in Fashion Island, the high end shopping mall in Newport Beach. The drive alone will take up the rest of the morning, and I suppose I could just as easily call her. Upon hearing my voice, she quite possibly will hang up on me or if she does stay on the line, I doubt she'll bother to tell me much. Seeing her in person will let me read her reaction, maybe even push the truth out of her, what exactly it was that she and my husband spoke about the other day, and why Grant chose to keep it from me.

◆

MOST MARRIAGES, IF THEY end abruptly with infidelity, have some noticeable fallout. Public backstabbing where one spouse turns all of the couples' friends against the other. Future retirement funds and 401K's half gutted. A long and costly divorce proceeding with multiple trips to the courthouse, then therapy sessions to unravel the psychological knot the former love of your life has left wadding bigger in your head by his or her inability to cut all ties, to just let you go.

But with Margaret, upon finding out her husband of thirty-six days was in love with another woman, there came an eerie silence. Some might attribute it to shock. Grant had shaken his head when I shared my doubts. "It's how she was raised. Keep your emotions in check at all times. Her father was a high level executive at an electric company. In his line of work vulnerability is an expensive weakness. Even her orgasms never rose an octave."

Margaret's clean way of ridding Grant from her life seemed like an obvious warning to me, meaning there would be greater repercussions later—cold strategizing to follow well after her husband settled into his new life with me. Grant claimed I was way off, but I know only too well the catastrophic tendencies of someone who no longer feels loved.

I've seen it in the shaky hands of my mother as she pointed the gun at the flesh canvas of my father's back before she steadied herself enough to pull the trigger. I've heard it in Martin's voice every time he calls or appears before me with some new damaging information he's unearthed to threaten or taunt me with about me or my family. It is exactly how I felt after I got the call about Grant's arrest for statutory rape. My heart made so much noise I could've taken a butcher knife to my chest just to make it stop. Before Grant made bail and his lawyer drove him home, I tossed the entire block of knives in the trash can outside. He never noticed they were missing. The trial consumed us. Evenings when we'd leisurely sipped wine for hours in the kitchen, chopping and sizzling colorful vegetables in a skillet to go with the lamb I had roasting in the oven have since been blanked out with white bags of lukewarm take-out.

The gallery is more of a hobby for Margaret than a business and she might not even be around today. It isn't like me not to think ahead, change my voice and pretend I am a customer. I could say that I need her expert knowledge of the complexities of the artworld before making my first big purchase. She'd believe it. I know she would. She never even noticed her husband had fallen for another woman at her own wedding.

Traffic is light until I switch freeways onto the 91. Only commuters with Fast Track passes get a break from the near twenty-four hour gridlock and breeze by in dark-windowed Range Rovers and Mercedes sedans in a private lane they pay through the nose to use freely. Once I get on the 55, I put the passenger's side window down a crack and take in the reassuring scent of the ocean seeping in.

I'm not so far away anymore.

Built like a Mediterranean style resort, Fashion Island overlooks the Pacific, one of the only shopping malls in the country with a view to die for. All economic levels are covered here from fifteen thousand dollar Louis Vuitton handbags at Neiman Marcus to sixty dollar boyfriend jeans at teenage friendly stores like Wet Seal and Urban Outfitters.

My cell goes off while I'm parking near Nordstrom, though I have no real idea where Margaret's gallery is located. Walking from shop to shop, burning off some of my anxiety at not knowing whether my husband is alive or dead might calm me before I pay a visit to his first wife. My father's name pops up at me on the tiny smart phone screen along with his number. This time it rings twice before he gives up. It isn't like me not to pick up for him. I will call him back after my visit with Margaret, before he pieces it together that something is very wrong.

Forever Blue sounds like the name of a greeting card shop, that is, if people still took the time to pen personal notes to each other instead of posting details of their lives every day on Facebook. Either Margaret is sending a cry for help over her perpetual dark state of mind or she wants her precious art gallery to sound like a denim store. Surprisingly, Margaret's gallery is closer to a Pretzel Hut than a shiny, high-priced department store. Polished hardwood floors and track lighting. Captured in the center of the room, under protective glass like a gift left for the art gods, sits a milky white sculpture of a weighty girl hunched over, her face distressed and her eyes oddly blurred. Price. Nine thousand dollars. Close to the amount of the down payment Grant and I scraped together for our two bedroom home. Margaret's wealth is just as abundantly on display as the ceramic girl.

"I have three signed prints from Ruscha."

It is Margaret's voice getting louder. She is coming back onto the floor. She was once Margaret Adams, her maiden name before she briefly became Margaret Jacobsen. Now she is Margaret Adams-Mirinetti, having married a retired Italian shipping magnate and realizing a hyphen is necessary in order not to lose her identity with each and every husband. Technically she and her senior citizen second husband are still newlyweds, married for around six months.

At first it sounds like she's talking to herself until I notice the tiny earpiece behind a diamond rock on her lobe. Her blond hair is shorter than I remember, a precise cut that angles toward her rounded chin. The last time I'd seen her was a chance run-in at a Japanese restaurant downtown. I was still a public defender. She was seated at a table alone, but by the menu left at the table setting across from her it was clear someone would be joining her. She'd nodded at me in a masculine way like two men might whose only connection was sex with a couple of the same women. There would be no small talk. Part of me wondered what she was doing so far away from her comfort zone, so close to mine. The courthouse was just one block in the other direction.

She has on a bright blue dress and zebra striped pumps, a color scheme I don't get but imagine must cost a fortune. Marriage to a magnate is showing in the deep tan she didn't get here in the thin winter Southern California sun. The color comes from a warmer exotic location somewhere below the equator. The hotel suite they stayed in was probably designed like a tiki hut that jutted out into the water with a glass floor to glimpse rare ocean life right underfoot. A five star Barbados resort she spotted on a travel channel is where she spent her honeymoon with Grant. It is hard to imagine Margaret having oily, sun-drenched sex with anyone.

Her blue eyes narrow in competitive assessment. It doesn't matter that she's remarried, she and I, as the former wife and the current one, permanently stand on separate sides of the same man—our common ground is our battleground. Margaret is not that surprised to see me. So well-manicured, she presents herself without fault, like a hostess greeting her guest of honor when I'm someone she would never include on any invitation list.

Before she gets the chance to see them, I drop my hands behind my back because of my clipped nails, the bruise on my arm I covered with make-up. Another fingernail has discolored, on the same hand, like I crushed it violently in a car door.

What have I done?

If Margaret knows that I should be in Palm Springs with Grant, she doesn't mention it. One of her beautiful hands flits gracefully to her chest, a spontaneous, even sincere expression of sympathy if I didn't know her better. People in her circle must buy this disingenuous act, they must buy her, including my husband whom I previously thought was a deeper judge of character. How else could it be explained why he still keeps in contact with such a shallow first wife?

"I'm so sorry about Grant's sentence," she says. "At the trial…"

"You were there?" Two large wooden courtroom doors closing come to mind, Grant's expression as he sat on the witness stand awaiting his turn at the truth, how his dark eyes recognized someone in the back before he or she left.

"No, no. I thought about going but decided against it. Not really my place. I guess an appeal is out of the question."

Already she is concealing from me the fact that Grant was thinking of calling her as a potential character witness. Is she playing me or does she really not know why I'm here?

"By the time a judge decides to even hear it, he'll be out of prison."

Given the seriousness of our conversation, Margaret's smile seems out of place, masking a certain level of condescension. Here, in her gleaming gallery, she must frequently use that smile on browsing customers whom she knows can't afford anything from her inventory, not even an empty frame. Margaret pities me.

"When you put it that way, his sentence doesn't seem so long, does it."

Twelve months is plenty long and she knows it.

"He didn't do it."

She sighs like she knows my husband so much better than I do. Apparently thirty-six days of marriage trumps my three years. How incredibly risky it would've been for Grant to trust her enough to allow her up on the stand as a character witness in his trial.

"He *was* convicted by a jury of his peers."

"Just because he had an affair and left you doesn't mean he slept with an underage girl."

Margaret fakes a laugh.

"Slept with, raped." She turns her hands palms up like she's literally weighing words. "Leave bride, marry whore, it's interesting how our Grant always finds himself between a rock and a hard place."

Her insults, her anger, are actually welcome. Her father would be very upset with her right about now. Her vulnerability, her weakness, is me.

"Is that why you called him the other day? To lend him this grand show of support?"

I've rattled her again. She wasn't expecting my sarcasm. She wasn't expecting me to know about the phone call. She must assume all of the conversations she has with her ex-husband are private. And even though most of them are, Grant has told me enough to make her want to blush with fury, like the fact she has low volume orgasms. She taps the toe of her high-heeled shoe so hard on the floor that a male assistant pops his head around the corner, a trendy horn-rimmed frame. He vanishes on sight with one sharp glance from her.

"Strange," Margaret says. "You and I—we're nothing alike yet we have two lovers in common."

She tilts her head back with a hand to her throat as if the words physically hurt as they come out. In the tunnel track lighting, her foundation is a shade lighter than the color of her neck. She must've just recently returned from her trip.

"We share two men, both of whom dumped me and for whatever reason can't seem to let you go."

Her eyes are now even with mine, and I notice a touch of black liner has smeared in one corner. Margaret takes a step closer to me. This is the closest I've ever seen her to losing her composure, letting anyone in on what she's really thinking.

"You need to be careful, Ava. You also need to leave *now*."

CHAPTER FOURTEEN

INSANITY

The Saturday before my thirteenth birthday my father broke the news that I'd be going to visit the woman who tried to kill him. "She's been asking about you, Kitsoli," was explanation enough as he wheeled out of my bedroom in his chair. He was acting like she was in rehab for an alcohol or eating addiction, not a mental institution for the criminally insane.

As far as I was concerned, I never wanted to see my mother again. She'd made me see too much. I've had to keep secrets. I could still hear the squeak of the screen door as my father swung it open and took one step outside. He'd nearly gotten away from her before the rapid pops. She'd shot straight through the mesh screen.

Word spread at school about my mother's arrest. Parental gossip can be the most destructive because the ugliness gets filtered through the mouth of a child. A girl with freckles named Tabitha, Tabby for short, like the cat, would heckle me in the lunch line.

"Ava's mom is a psy–cho," she'd say with a singsong head tilt, ear to ear as she drew out the syllables.

Her two friends laughed, creepy blonde twin girls who were getting a little too old at twelve for high parted pigtails. Most of the time I kept my back to them, I ignored them the way my father told me to. Except for one time I found I couldn't any longer. I'd heard their taunts for long enough.

I turned and caught Tabitha stabbing the air like she was holding a knife while she chanted the tired truth, "Ava's mom is a psy—cho, Ava's mom is a psy—cho."

I'm not sure what got into me, at least that is what I told the lunch monitor, the principal and later my father after he was called.

I'd show Freckle Girl what psycho is. With my arm extended, I pointed my index finger, thumb up, like a pistol, her face my bull's eye.

Her identical sidekicks ditched her fast, scattering from the line.

Tabitha stood alone, her eyes a little cross-eyed from staring at my makeshift gun, her mouth still open in mid-chant.

I fired.

"Pow," I said. *"That's how she did it."*

◆

COURTROOMS AND PRISON LIFE weren't in my mother's future. On the night of her arrest she'd been placed in a holding cell with only one cellmate, a prostitute. My mother went to work. Using only her teeth, she tore a long strip of denim off the pant leg of her jeans. In her struggle, a gold crown was swallowed and her jaw came loose, an injury that would require her mouth to be wired shut for weeks. But none of that mattered. The prostitute, mistakenly egged my mother on, thinking she was about to watch a live suicide. If anything, my mother was consistent in her belief in one thing—every woman she came across had slept with my father.

It took two male guards to cut the prostitute down from the top bar of the cell where she flailed for life and clutched at the lethal collar that kept tightening around her throat. My mother sat calmly on the bench, the dangling woman just a few feet away. She must've been aware in some recess of her mind that by pulling this stunt she'd just gotten herself off the hook for another attempted murder, the one that actually meant something, her very own husband.

Police investigators and one friendly psychologist interviewed me several times after the shooting. Between sweet sips of Coke or Sprite, they tried to coax the truth out of me. No matter how many times I told them that my mother had grabbed the Berretta 32 out of my father's sock drawer, they all seemed to jot down the same thing in their notes. Ruled too sick in the head to stand trial, my mother was to shuffle in slippers indefinitely around a mental hospital. I thought it was unfair for her to be moving at all since thanks to her my father now had a pair of dead legs.

The bullet she fired into my father's back was left lodged

in his spine, the damage already done. After he was discharged from the hospital, a metal ramp was fixed to our porch steps. Every Monday and Thursday a female nurse named Edna with man hands came by to help my father bathe and prepare our meals for the rest of the week pre portioned out in Tupperware containers inside the fridge.

Other things in our house changed too. I did all of the laundry and nothing was stored anymore in the higher cabinets above the kitchen counter.

As a cop my father used to wrestle suspects twice his strength, tripping on PCP, straight to the ground but now he had trouble using a hand held claw with a skinny extension designed as a long metal arm. It was supposed to reach the unreachable but proved useless to grab anything heavy or boxy in shape for very long. After my father dropped a pickle jar and scattered Goldfish crackers all over the kitchen linoleum, he buried the device in the trash, too humiliated to try it again. In case he might change his mind, Edna fished the device out of the garbage and hid it coincidentally in a place he'd never look, one of the higher cabinets. My father never did.

◆

THE CAB DRIVER, a guy in his fifties, who reminded me of a trucker, waited for us on the curb, smoking a cigarette. He wore a black T-shirt and on his forearms were old tattoos that had blurred with age. The back passenger door of the cab was flung open. It was mid-July and the heat in the Valley scorched past a hundred degrees yet my father insisted I wear my nice black cashmere sweater I wore at Christmas because my mother liked it on me, the color of death.

My father came first down the ramp, rolling toward the taxi because it would take longer for him to get settled in the backseat. The driver was quick to glance away, to stamp out his cigarette and then pop the trunk.

It was an impossible hate I felt for my mother every time I caught that same fleeting expression on a new stranger's face—a mixed look of pity and curiosity at the handicapped man, my father, who would always be viewed as a paraplegic before a person.

Visiting hours at Shadow Hills were only from 1:30 p.m. to 3:30 p.m., though two hours with my mother seemed far too long. What was I supposed to say to her— *Thanks for being a bad shot, Mom. Or else I'd be orphaned with no parents.* According to hospital guidelines, my arms and fingers must be bare. On the car ride over my father even slipped out the rubber band in my hair because he wanted to make sure everything ran smoothly. He wanted to make sure I saw her.

The outside of the hospital resembled a prison. Barbed wire was coiled across the tops of chain link that outlined the boundaries of the facility and a security guard manned the booth at the gate. The guard leaned down as my father lowered his window.

"Ava Nicoli here to see Iris Nicoli."

Having our names strung together made me sound like her accomplice. I was my father's daughter, not hers. I was the one who took the gun out of her hand. I was the one who called 911. There were other things, too, left out of the police report that my father and I never spoke about.

We were waved in and a woman in a pant suit met us curbside at the front of a one story building that spread out in all different directions practically like the Pentagon. Her hair was pulled back tight but I liked her smile. Her handshake was warm.

"I'm Dr. Livingston," she said. "You must be Ava."

She turned to my father.

"She is gorgeous. I'll be the one taking her to see Iris."

I panicked and let go of the woman's hand.

"Dad, I thought you were coming in with me."

My father looked straight ahead as if he had to.

"Seeing me might jeopardize her recovery, *Kitsoli*."

Dr. Livingston was now in control. My father was parroting her words. We were on her turf and she closed the cab and I watched it depart until the back of my father's head was out of sight. He never once turned back to look at me. Inside the hospital patients wore baggy gray sweatshirts and matching sweatpants. There was a recreation room with a large TV turned off and some empty couches. Everything smelled like bleach and cafeteria food when no kitchen was visible. Two women with hair combed straight and unstyled crouched over a table playing backgammon. Neither one of them looked up from their game when we passed by the room. I wondered what atrocious acts they were in for and if their loved ones whom they'd most likely terrorized actually came to see them.

In a crazy place like this everything was turned around. It wasn't about the life or death of the innocent victims. In here the perpetrators of unspeakable violence were simply called patients. They were talked to, soothed, rewarded with hot food and fold-out board games.

"Everybody is outside playing softball," Dr. Livingston explained. "We try and appreciate the beautiful sunny days."

My mother sat on the edge of a single bed in a room that looked like a college dorm. There was space for another bed but seeing my mother's history with roommates I'm sure Dr. Livingston knew better than to give her one. My mother wore the same sweatpants as the others. A pair of slip-on Keds with no shoelaces were on her feet. Her thick black hair was pulled back at the sides in barrettes, making her look young even though she was well into her forties. Her hands were folded neatly in her lap, and I saw the wedding band she dared to still wear on her finger. Maybe it was all the jewelry she was allowed to wear. She could've been a plain clothes soccer mom caught running errands. That was the danger of my mother, how normal and harmless she first appeared.

"There's my pretty girl," she exclaimed. "I forgot how much you look like me." She clapped her hands together. Her fingernails were trimmed the way I still keep mine, for strength. Only weak hysterical women scratched each other's eyes out.

Typical of my mother, she slid a compliment for herself in there too. She made no show of physical affection toward me. She didn't even get up off the bed. The absence of her hug hurt and then came the stinging glare that lasted only seconds. In the seven months since her arrest my waist had narrowed and I'd filled out; now I was wearing a bra.

Later as an adult I understood that look to be aimed at a romantic rival, not a daughter. It was the look Grant's ex-wife gave me or any nameless woman hanging off Martin's arm, naive enough to think she had a real future with him. . Maybe my mother really was crazy.

With Dr. Livingston well out of earshot, I found myself getting comfortable in my new position. I went so far as to sit beside my mother on the bed. Somewhere in a coffee shop nearby my father was waiting out this visit in the hopes there would be more to follow. It angered me how much he was still trying to make things right, to construct some semblance of family with a woman who wanted him dead. It would be up to me at thirteen to be the one who blew our family apart once and for all.

"Dad is in love with someone else," I whispered, grabbing my mother's hand. "She's already moved in."

I looked over at Dr. Livingston. Her expression beamed pure progress at the reunion between my mother and me. My mother's dark eyes were my eyes, and I wondered if she could tell I was lying. I squeezed her hand hard to keep the upper hand.

"If you ever ask to see me again, I'm going to tell them everything. You'll never get out of here."

Three weeks later while my father and I were finishing off a box of pepperoni pizza for dinner, he got the call that abruptly put a stop to the routine pattern of our lives once again.

My mother was last seen in the bleachers watching a softball game between two teams of playful nut jobs. She detested all sports but no one at the facility knew that. Somehow she was able to sneak away long enough to crack the skull of a female janitor and steal her uniform. The poor woman would need thirteen stitches and eye surgery to reattach the retina.

Nobody knew for sure how my mother did it, how she managed to walk right out of a maximum security mental hospital without anyone noticing. The staff, including Dr. Livingston, assumed responsibility for my mother's escape when really the awful truth of who was to blame lied solely on me.

CHAPTER FIFTEEN

BUILD-UP

My navy blue Volkswagon Passat sits parked in the driveway of our home in Studio City like this is any other weekday and my husband hasn't been missing for close to forty-eight hours. Around this time of day, before the trial, I would be in the kitchen trying out some new quick and easy dish I'd found on the Internet or if Grant called and said he'd be late, I'd curl up on the couch with a glass of Merlot, prepping for classes or grading papers. At four in the afternoon, thanks to fall back hours, the sky is practically dusk. No children are out playing on the sidewalks being yelled at by their parents to come indoors, still hours shy of the 9 to 5 nightly joggers who dart in and out of sight in their reflective workout gear.

Routine is the pulse of any neighborhood and I'm nearly convinced I can pull off entering my own home without being seen, having driven here in the wrong car.

Mrs. Wilkes in the knee-length housecoat might be a problem. She is staring at me from across the street, a couple houses down, a limp garden hose in her hand. As an eyewitness, I could blindside her. First, since Grant and I moved in, she's had a stroke or two. Her vision is faulty and at eighty-one so is her mind. If pressed, I'm sure I could convince her she got the dates mixed up of when she saw me drive up in my husband's car when I'm supposed to be on vacation. She doesn't know I'm supposed to be away, but the cops would inform her should it come to that.

A small white mini-truck, the useless kind that can't haul much more than a couple of 2 X 4's, inches by before speeding up, the driver apparently mistaking the directions. Construction work is constantly going on in our neighborhood—new pools, another room addition, maybe even a small guesthouse. Only a few miles from Universal Studios, movie people with high paying jobs who want to live like the rest of us plant roots here. They spend so much money improving their homes they may as well have plunked down the cash upfront for a bigger spread hidden up in a curve on Laurel Canyon Boulevard.

Mrs. Wilkes sets down the hose, now fussing over a bed of daffodils. Too much time has been spent focusing on a nosy old widow.

I face the reason why I'm back. I face my house, the porch steps, the clay potted cactus on the top step with its one stiff blooming pink flower Grant bought me because everything I attempt to grow withers no matter the amount of sunlight or how often I water it. Envelopes peek out of the mailbox. The welcome mat is slightly askew like someone, maybe the mailman, turned too fast on it after dropping off our bills.

The sadness is overwhelming, it's bone deep. For once I'm not expecting my husband to come home. I don't know for sure if he's even still alive. But I want to believe it. I have to believe it. My only other option is to just give in and let the law take everything from the life of my husband to all the time we've spent loving each other inside this house.

Our one story made of brick is just the way we bought it and reminds me of a New England cottage with its white shutters, matching French doors and hardwood floors. Grant and I have been content here in this quaint house that looks nothing like the others. For the three years we've lived here we've kept to ourselves. We aren't unfriendly to our neighbors but we don't strike up small talk with them either. No spontaneous invitations for a block barbecue. We've never needed more than each other for company, for backyard rib eye steaks grilled to perfection on a warm night or a cozy night in by the fireplace.

I've returned home because I have to. The slim chance remains that he's found a way out of the desert and there it is, like the image of him hanging by a bed sheet outside the hotel balcony, this time he's positioned on our bed, his arms at his sides, foam from his insides spilling out of his mouth. The thought of his suicide jumbles me up and it takes me two tries with the key to unlock the front door.

Inside the house it's dark except for the red blinking light of the answering machine that rests on an end table. I play back the four messages, a delay tactic to hold off on confirming my fears of what lies behind our bedroom door. Remote possibility, yes, but Grant could've called the house instead of my cell. He's told me more than once that I've changed my cell number too many times for him to remember it offhand.

"Hey, Ava. Connie here. Just letting you know the next department meeting is this coming Friday at three." Connie is my boss, the childless, husbandless department chair whose idea of pets are a couple of brainless canaries because she pretty much lives at the university. There is always that awkward silence from the people I know who have been following the trial. What does one say to a woman whose husband is a convicted rapist? If I were on Connie's end, I wouldn't know either. "Hope to see you there," she adds as filler for a goodbye.

Next.

"Grant." It is Reynolds, his voice weighted down by alcohol or defeat. One of the reasons why Grant hired Reynolds had been his winning reputation. "There's a couple things we need to discuss before we meet down at the courthouse Monday."

Right, I think. Before my husband gets shackled at the wrists, then strip searched and you send me the bill for it.

Grant has nothing more to say to this shyster unless it's about a costly appeal that won't make a difference anyway. I was telling the truth to Margaret earlier about how long it would take for the appeal to surface. Unless more evidence was presented, a new judge would rule Grant received a fair trial. Our savings were zeroed out over one witness, one seventeen year old girl who cried more than she said anything credible and Grant was dealt the maximum twelve month sentence. Her tears proved so convincing that the judge stipulated she didn't want Grant getting out early due to overcrowding. That point was for show really since her word would not mean much once Grant was actually in prison.

I play back the message. The call from Reynolds came in a little after ten-thirty this morning. He has Grant's cell phone number and if he starts calling and not getting an answer, he could make trouble. I wouldn't put it past him to save his own skin by alerting the bail bondsmen or the court.

The last message is silence, a long pause like the one I received the night before, the same unknown caller using a throwaway phone. Then the line goes dead. Only this time the person calls back mere seconds later, not to leave a message but to check that nobody is home. This last call came in less than fifteen minutes ago.

I look around the room and realize I'm still standing in the dark, vulnerable to the shadows that could be concealing anything from a high-backed chair to a human form. How reckless of me to think I might be safe in my own home. Outside something jingles—a dog on a walk with its owner.

Was the caller here now? Hiding out between some overcoats in the hall closet or a few feet away behind the swinging kitchen door? Hastily, I flip on a switch and the hallway lights up leading to the study and the bedroom. I turn on my cell that's in my pocket in case I get ambushed, in case I have the chance during the struggle to dial 911.

The floorboards creak with every step, giving me away. It is not too late for me to make a break for the front door. But I don't. As with every rational thought I've had these past few months, I discard it, and I keep moving toward the bedroom door. My husband could be lying lifeless in our bed, proof he was remorseful for betraying me, the woman whom he's called in every anniversary card or gift tag on every present, the love of his life. I used to think they were more than the right words a husband is supposed to label his wife with. I used to think he actually lived and breathed them for me until I got that devastating call about his arrest.

A part of me would rather find him dead of an overdose than to know for certain that he forced himself on a seventeen-year-old girl.

The bedroom door is shut and I can't remember if I had left it that way. I had been the last to lock up and leave the house. Grant had an appointment with Reynolds before we made the trip down to Palm Springs and I'd met him in the driveway, afraid if he came back inside the house to get me I might lose my nerve and want to stay home. For close to a year now our marriage has been peopled with a double-wide lawyer, his secretaries and paralegals, all of whom had kept us from being alone with each other for any real length of time.

With one hand on my phone, I use the other to turn the knob and then move to the nightstand and switch on the table lamp on Grant's side of the bed.

Thankfully there is no body on the bed. Our down comforter is stretched flat and stuffed, the way I'd made it before I packed for our trip. Our matching nightstands are bare with only a table lamp and a cordless phone on Grant's side which we never use. No books, no remote controls, no laptops. We rarely read before bed. We don't even have a TV in here.

Sleep and sex.

Our bedroom used to really be that simple.

I check our walk-in closet. Nothing is out of place except for the four inch black heels I kicked off at the last minute. I had thought I was just going to the desert for a few days of relaxation. There had been no plans to seduce my husband, to follow him to our bungalow and to climax so easily with him after so long. I'd purposely made a point of slipping my feet into flat sandals, the kind Grant didn't care to see me in. His side of the closet is neatly aligned in sections—business shirts, dress pants, suit jackets, some still in the plastic dry cleaning wrap. Ten pairs of leather shoes, one pair of bright white running shoes for the gym. My side, compared to his, is a disaster, with summer dresses mixed in with pencil skirts and blouses I wear to teach.

Grant's organizational skills are methodical which will make him much harder to locate. The fear of an intruder is fading fast because if there was someone in the house he would've attacked me by now. My back has been turned to the rest of the house for some time. Due to all the shootings on college campuses I started carrying pepper spray on my keychain. No help to me now since Grant's keys are in my hand, so is his cell phone. I must've left my things back in the car.

The next place I look is in the study. My laptop is on the expensive hand crafted oak desk, the only piece of furniture Grant insisted on taking in the divorce with Margaret. Grant's tablet is usually in a book bag hanging off the side of the desk chair. During the investigation our home computer was confiscated by the police, the hard drive inspected. Minus a couple of porn sites, Grant proved himself to be no online predator. Neither one of us had the stomach to pick up the computer from the evidence room since it really was no longer ours. Instead we both bought totable computers, another means of detachment from one another. He might've chosen to contact me this way to avoid an immediate response.

I find a message about the department meeting which Connie called about is listed in the subject header. Among the others clogging my email, I scroll down through the junk mail, professors either cheap or just hard up for cash selling children's bicycles, a gently used size eight pair of two inch heels, or weekend ski tickets to Big Bear.

Another message is from Helen Larkin, no one I've ever heard of. A personal Google account. She's casually friendly in her greeting as if we know each other.

Hi Ava,

I just want you to know I'm willing to forgive the cost of a new phone if you agree to meet me…

The unstylish blogger in the skirt and running shoes whose wrist I held down in toilet water. Humiliating her in that way had very little effect. Trying to extort an interview out of me over a ruined phone is ridiculous, another rookie move. A real reporter would've approached me differently, without the awkward confrontation in a women's restroom or the follow-up email. I delete the message because she's the least of my worries.

I scroll some more.

An email pops up as spam, but its subject header is what strikes me, the letter V over and over again— Grant's nickname for me.

My heart speeds up, and I don't care about the warning that it's unsecured and could be a virus. The message has to be from my husband, and I click on it. He might've sent the email from an address he came up with on the fly at a coffee house or an Apple store. The message is cryptic and lasts all of one line:

What's for dinner?

It came in hours ago, well before the hang up calls. I snap closed the computer and glance back out at the open door. Had I thought to lock all the doors before I left for our trip? After I unlocked the front door this afternoon it didn't occur to me to check the rear one that led to the backyard. There could be a square of broken glass from the French door, evidence reflecting all over the dining room floor of a break-in. No man in a ski mask ever showed himself on someone's front porch for all the neighbors to see.

Was Grant playing some kind of twisted joke on me, acting on his resentment because I never firmly said I believed in his innocence? For a moment I close my eyes because what he said to me shortly after his arrest is becoming as important to me as our vows. I want to believe him now as I did then he was telling me the truth. "I would never cheat on you, V. You're the woman I see every time I close my eyes when we're fucking. *You are my fantasy.*"

From room to room, I flip on every goddamn light in the house. I don't expect this to be some kind of movie where I find a small animal boiling in a pot on the stove, but I know there's more than just an email this person has left for me to find. In the kitchen I grab a stainless steel skillet, not very effective if the person in my home is armed with a knife or a gun.

In the dining room where Grant and I had pushed around so much take-out with our forks, is a place setting for two—China plates I've never seen before, heavy silverware, and champagne flutes. The centerpiece is a heavy crystal vase filled with a dozen white roses, clipped symmetrically at the stems.

Martin used to have bouquets of them sent to my office at the courthouse. Although beautiful the petals seemed like the color was bled out of them, especially when they came in long strands inside a bright gold box. There was never a card attached. Part of his power pump was that the gesture alone would be enough to know they were from him. A couple of times after he found out that Grant had left his childhood friend and moved in with me, Martin continued to have the flowers sent to my office, not caring who might've caught on. Typically they arrived after I'd won a case as if they marked a celebration. When a bouquet appeared in my new office at the university once word got back to him I'd quit being a public defender, I knew the roses had taken on a new meaning. He wasn't going to let me get away so easily.

Martin was toying with me now because he could. If I report a break-in there will be no prints found on the vase. It will be his word against mine. With my recent emotional turmoil of a husband on trial for rape, Martin's word will carry greater weight. He was Judge Durham. He even has a cute redhead court reporter to point to as proof that he's long since moved on from old feelings for me. I've made a big mistake in not realizing the lengths Martin will go to get what he wants. His arrogance would insist that he do it all himself so there would be no errors. Given his criminal contacts it wouldn't be hard for him to get a driver's license made with his photo and Grant's information on it. Pay off a doctor who is already on the take to phony up a prescription. Martin is a man who personally metes out punishment whether it's in his courtroom or elsewhere. In my rush to find out if the prescription of Seconal had been picked up, I hadn't thought to ask the girl at the pharmacy what the man who retrieved the pills looked like.

CHAPTER SIXTEEN

JEALOUSY

G rant never came by my gym. Too impatient for a chance encounter, he boldly called my office ten days after meeting me as if it was his right to see me again, as if a relationship between us had already started. I was in court for two of his calls which made it appear like I was ignoring him or playing games. The phone messages he left with my assistant included his first name only and the reason check box on the business message pad was marked "personal."

When I did return his call I appeared to reach his actual cell number because I heard his voice on the voicemail, a friendly sounding message yet curt enough to be appropriate for business contacts. It surprised me that he hadn't thought far enough ahead to buy a disposable phone. Already he was in for it with his wife if she was the one who paid the monthly bills.

I didn't leave a message but my work number must've showed up on his list of recent calls because he called me right back.

"Meet me for coffee," Grant said. There was confidence in his voice. He knew I'd taken the biggest step of all by calling him back.

I may as well have shown up at his office in nothing but a black fur coat and bright red heels.

"Coffee?"

"Yes," he said again. "Coffee."

I let the silence say the rest. Coffee houses are a far riskier place for two people who are attracted to one another to meet than a bar. A well lit room with comfortable chairs and close tables meant he wanted to get to know me better first. It scared me to think that this could be more than just a brief thing where miraculously no one got hurt. And yet I had just broken up with Martin on the off chance Grant would get in touch with me again. Still, one of us in a committed relationship was complication enough.

"Ava? You there?"

I moved files around like things were hectic. Every part of me longed to see him again, but it kept nagging at me. What kind of a man seeks out another woman when he's a newlywed? Before I could answer my own question, I found myself answering his.

"I can be there after four."

Over the buzz of baristas shouting out triple Lattes and extra pumps of espresso, I heard Grant call out my name from the line. He was in a suit without the jacket, casually more attractive in his own clothes than the rented tux at his wedding reception. The only indication that he was recently married was the color in his face. He and Margaret must've gone to a tropical locale for their honeymoon because the last couple of weeks had been overcast, especially by the beaches.

It was in Grant's eyes, how happy he was to see me again, literally lifted up which seemed strange. With a bride in the wings I was expecting him to look torn. He'd looked pretty convincingly in love with her when he took her in his arms out on the dance floor at their reception.

Grant eyed the drink menu.

"You strike me as a black coffee, black. No sugar, no mocha. Definitely no cream."

I nodded.

"If I wanted all that extra sweet stuff I'd order chocolate milk."

As he paid for our two black coffees I noticed his left hand was missing a gold band. I wondered if it was stashed in his pants pocket or the console of his car.

We picked the most private table in the house, next to a young Asian guy on his computer, wearing ear buds. When Grant sat down, he rolled up his sleeves, as though preparing to dig up to the elbows to find out everything about me. His interest unnerved me.

I'd have to be careful. I told him about my father being a former police officer from Burbank and how he'd been on disability because of a shooting. Grant assumed the rest, that it was work related, a thief or some other criminal lowlife who somehow got the drop on a seasoned police officer and was able to shoot him in the back. I preferred having Grant think my father was a bumbling cop than the victim of his own wife's homicidal rage.

No matter how understanding Grant was coming off, I couldn't bear to see the change in his face once I told him the truth about my mother. I'd seen the look before. He was my boyfriend in law school, in his third year and I was in my first year at UCLA. We'd met in the library where he was boning up on California tax codes and I was doing case research for a paper I was writing on the soft sentences for drunk drivers who commit vehicular homicide. He was fraternity boy attractive, a sporty guy with a round face and sunny blond hair, who looked like his face might never change shape, never mature with the lines and contours of an adult.

We turned out to be more study partners than lovers, curled up with our bulky law books in an old leather recliner, the back cushion peeling, in the apartment on campus he shared with two other roommates. He was ordinary in bed, always killing the mood afterward by talking of marriage, children, what private schools our children would attend, the starter home we'd buy in Glendale before our law careers took off and we could afford a roomy home fit for a family in affluent Hancock

Park. But he was steady, a sure thing in every sense of the word.

That is, until one of his roommates informed him about my mother. "It isn't that I don't love you with all my heart," he'd said when he told me we'd need to slow down. "It's just that I don't know if I want to chance *my children* inheriting that gene. We'll need to do some research on it."

The next day I stopped returning his calls, relieved I was no longer in a relationship that sounded more like a science experiment. My mother became my excuse, my reason to run and I did just that running away from any man who wanted more from me than a brief, no strings relationship.

Like mother like daughter. It was a beloved cliché embroidered on pillows. I no longer even knew where Iris was or if she was even still alive. No one knew. After a few years the people who cared at the mental hospital stopped trying to look for her, they changed jobs or like Dr. Livingston, retired. My mother became a cold case file with the LAPD, if they hadn't lost her file or it had been destroyed. Everyone assumed she'd probably wandered off somewhere and killed herself. Grant would nod at all this and pretend he was listening, but all he'd be thinking about would be the time and how he needed to get the hell out of here, away from me. Margaret here he comes. After one coffee with me he'd never think of straying again. I pictured him laughing with his friends, saying, "I guess you could say I dodged a damn bullet!"

So I turned the subject to him and what was safe to talk about, his life before Margaret. I learned about Grant's fractured family, how they lived three thousand miles away in Maryland. His father was a lobbyist for an environmental organization, his mother a housewife who made her own granola. His capitalistic choice for a career must've been what led him so far away from home when Lower Manhattan and the financial district was the closer, obvious place for an investment banker.

"Why are you a public defender?" he asked. "Seems to me prosecutors get the respectability and defense lawyers in private practice get the big money. What exactly do you get?"

It was a fair question that felt more personal to ask then which position I preferred during sex. On any given day either question would be hard for me to answer. Sometimes I don't know why I do the things I do. I said what sounded best.

"I represent criminals who slip through the cracks. Rapists and murderers get pro bono high profile defense teams. But what does the eighteen-year-old gang member who sold some dope to an undercover cop get?"

Grant smiled, amused. He covered my hand with his.

"He should get what he deserves. Prison time."

Grant's fingers were long and slender, sexually distracting the way a woman's bare legs might be to a man. I had on a skirt and I imagined him driving one or two of them inside me, manipulating me into a climax without my having to take off a stitch of clothing.

Grant's thumb stroked the inside of my palm. He was quiet, looking at me, possibly thinking of his next move.

It was close to dinner time, an hour when a new wife will start calling so I made the next move. I slipped my hand out from under his and made the excuse I had somewhere I needed to go.

Something crossed Grant's face quickly, irritation maybe. "Dinner with the judge?"

I shook my head, thinking twice about telling Grant we'd broken up. It would seem like I was too eager to start something with him and might scare him off. Up until then it sounded like we were old friends catching up. Within seconds I was turning into a holdout, a tease who played one guy against the other when I always hated that girl. *I wasn't that girl.* I thanked Grant for the two dollar coffee that went cold a half hour ago and I left unsure if I'd ever see him again.

One evening a few days later my assistant had just left for the day when Grant suddenly filled the doorway, all six feet of him.

I glanced down at his empty hands, expecting he'd at least have brought take-out as an excuse. But Grant was a man who didn't like to make many of them, excuses, that is, nor was he the type like Martin to rest his head in my lap to initiate sex. This man simply locked the door.

For some women his aggressiveness might be cause for alarm, but I wasn't worried. I wasn't about to be raped. He would've let me out if I asked. Soon he had me pressed up against the wall. The force sent my framed law degree from UCLA sliding down, the glass cracked from my elbow. I was probably bleeding but didn't care.

Our first kiss was smooth and deep, and I got a sense that Grant had been practicing how this first time would play out. Already he knew me well enough not to suggest a hotel or to come over to my apartment. Either scenario would remind me of the reason why we couldn't do this at his place.

Over his shoulder I glimpsed a shadow blocking the bar of light from the space under the front door of my office. Someone was standing right outside. It could've been anyone who heard my body against the wall, then the crash of broken glass. The throes of heated sex was not so different from the sounds of a break-in. The person on the other side listening in could be a custodian, someone who had a master key and would unknowingly walk in on the sight of a half naked public defender whose skirt had just been tossed somewhere on the other side of her desk.

"I'm working late," I managed. "Please come back another time."

Grant froze, his warm hand caught between the cup of my bra and my breast. The person stood there for an unbearably long moment before moving on. Well after the fact I would remember there was no noise of a cleaning cart full of supplies that accompanied the footsteps. The soles of the shoes sounded hard on the floor and did not have the rubber squeak common with the cleaning crew.

It had been a Tuesday night and the custodians only came around on Mondays and Thursdays.

◆

GRANT LEFT MARGARET FOR me a month after marrying her, after he was certain he and I were sexually compatible. I didn't fault Grant for that. Most men put sex above all else in a relationship. Sharing, conversation and friendship all were a faraway second. My one bedroom apartment in Burbank was too small for us to stay in for long. Grant showed up with only a small suitcase, a garment bag full of suits. He wasn't so impressed with the view I had of the parking lot of a midscale hotel that catered to tourists. Every morning a double decker red bus swung by and people in sun visors and baseball caps rode on the roof to snap pictures of the front gates and ivy covered walls outside of celebrity homes. Most of the time Grant kept the drapes closed. The sight must've been depressing. He'd come from a spacious house with the ocean practically at his feet.

We both had a thing for Chinese food and Mexican and movies, any kind. Grant loved the corny action types with explosions and predictable endings. We shared a bucket of popcorn and made up for the fact our first kiss ended in sex by making out with buttery mouths in the back row of the theater throughout most of the films we paid to see. We had done things backward by getting serious before getting to know each other, and it was Grant who heard about it the most.

At night in bed we'd talk, my back to him while he handled my waist as if getting used to the dimensions of a new woman.

"I got another call telling me I'm crazy for leaving."

"Yeah? Who this time?"

"My mother."

"You told your parents?"

"Margaret called them." Grant's laugh had a hard edge to it. "She assumed they have some influence on me. Shows how little she ever knew me."

"If you want to go back…"

"I don't." Grant fit his hand between my thighs. It wasn't a ploy for sex. He found comfort falling asleep with his hand in the softest place on my body the way a person might press their hands next to their cheek. "Jesus, V. I was just trying to tell you how stupid they're all being. They don't get that we're real. There is no going back. What is it going to take for you to believe me?"

"I believe you."

But my words sounded insincere even to me. I have always been a terrible liar.

Several days later while Grant and I were checking out affordable homes, he told me to check the mailbox. We were at the fifth listing we'd been to that day, the two bedroom cottage in Studio City. The black metal box was attached to the front of the house inches beside the door. The postman with this route had a bit of a walk each day.

I didn't get it.

"What do you mean, check the mail?"

Grant smiled, partly in shadow from the shade of an oak tree on the front lawn that looked generations older than the house.

"You didn't know? A Mrs. Nicoli-Jacobsen lives here."

I lifted the lid and reached inside, touching on a small box most likely from a jewelry store.

The proposal was original, at least by my standards. No ring at the bottom of a fizzing glass of champagne. Grant didn't get down on one knee. But the staging of it all still took my breath away. In one afternoon with the help of one mailbox Grant literally delivered me my future.

◆

THE FIRST SIGN MARTIN wasn't taking our break up well came in the form of four slashed tires. My car was parked in the courthouse lot when it happened yet as populated as it was with attorneys, defendants, plaintiffs and other disgruntled citizens cattle called in for jury duty, nobody saw a thing. There were no security cameras outside, only inside the courtroom halls.

At a little after five, the lot was emptying out. Grant was at his divorce attorney's office signing all of his marital assets away to Margaret who promised in return she'd give him an annulment. If leaving a woman after a month of marriage didn't constitute fraud, Margaret's attorney claimed, she wasn't sure what did. Possibly the tire damage was a parting gift from Margaret, but she'd done nothing so far, not even place one vengeful call to me. She relinquished Grant as if he was a lease whose time had run out.

The deflated tires caused my car to be several inches shorter than the rest in the row and I had to bend down low in order to peer in through the driver's side window. Nothing appeared to have been taken and there were no insulting words scratched into the dash. The perpetrator apparently was interested in making a statement, a costly and inconvenient one. Grant was under enough stress so I simply called a tow service and waited. As I paced beside my squat car, I racked my mind trying to come up with a client, a distraught family member of a client, a victim, anyone who would be mad enough to take a knife to each and every tire and risk being seen doing it. Lately my cases had all been pretty routine, with deals made with the prosecution before trials ever began. For the past six months I'd had no emotionally wrought rape or murder cases. No gory gang initiation drive-bys.

"Hey," a voice called out from across the lot. "What the hell happened?"

It was Martin with a briefcase in hand and a concerned look on his face. By this time a tow truck was backed close against the tail end of my car and the tower was lowering the ramp.

I shrugged.

"Tire trouble."

Martin whistled.

"You must've set off the wrong person. This looks pretty personal."

There was something in the way he said this last line about it being personal that made me feel uneasy. Months back when I'd told him face to face I needed some time to myself, Martin recognized it for what it was—a bad attempt at saying I wanted out of our relationship.

Martin grabbed my hand, then kissed my cheek and kept me close. His voice was a whisper. "I think a little time is what you'll need to see just how right we are for each other."

A couple of days after that exchange, I received a bouquet of white roses from Martin which I took as an apology for overstepping. Since then he'd smiled at me in the halls, asking me out to lunch once or twice which I had yet to take him up on.

Most spurned exes who commit acts of vandalism stick around to witness the reaction their destruction has caused on the person they won't let go of. If Martin was behind it I wasn't about to give him the satisfaction of looking spooked.

"It's just a lot of rubber," I said. "Easily replacable."

Martin's cell went off but he clicked it quiet immediately without checking the number.

"Obviously you need a lift."

I shook my head.

"Thanks, but I'll ride with the driver."

"You'd rather ride with white trash than with me?"

Martin's outburst caused the tow truck driver to look up from shackling my car. Instantly I felt bad for him in his coveralls and his greasy hands that would never get the grime out no matter how many times he scrubbed them. He looked like a hard worker, probably had a wife and kids at home. Martin could care less that he offended the guy, not bothering to look in his direction, much less apologize. He wasn't going to let up until he got me in his white Volvo.

It seemed excessive to own two cars for different times of the week. I was angry someone of his stature would act this crazy and stoop this low.

"Let me drive you home, Ava."

"It's really out of your way," I said.

I knew how it would look if Grant saw me being dropped off by my former boyfriend, and I wasn't falling for that trap. Grant and I were in love. We were clearing the slates of anyone who could get in our way. Escrow closed and he and I had moved into the cottage with practically no furniture just the cramped double bed, a loveseat, the office desk and a table and chairs from my apartment. We would slowly rebuild, filling our home with new things, the way most new couples did.

I climbed up into the passenger side of the tow truck, not about to look back at Martin still standing there in the parking lot. He might see for sure that I knew it was him, that I knew he was probably carrying the knife he'd slashed the tires of my car with concealed in the briefcase he held in his hand.

◆

DURING THE CHRISTMAS PARTY later that year, Martin came up to me at the free bar. He was engaged now to a knockout real estate agent in her late twenties. She was associated with a lucrative company and her glamour shot was plastered on billboards all across LA freeways. Knowing Martin it was how they first met. He was sitting in his car stuck in traffic, liked what he saw and dialed.

"So how does it feel to be a newlywed?" he asked. The syllables of his words ran into the next. He sounded a little drunk.

I looked over at Grant who was standing with my assistant Monica and her live-in girlfriend. Lesbians and straight women are all the same when it comes to chatting at a man and rarely letting him get in a word.

Grant took a sip of his Heineken, nodding here and there, politely keeping eye contact when his mind had to be elsewhere. We'd been married on Thanksgiving weekend, standing precariously near a cliff in Big Sur with only my father as family in attendance and Monica and her girlfriend as witnesses.

"It feels good," I said. The bartender poured more champagne in my glass. Talk of Grant might send Martin and I to a bad place—the courthouse parking lot that evening after my tires had been slashed. "I should get back to him."

Martin took my glass and set it and his tumbler of whiskey on the rocks down on the bar counter. He was in a black suit and a black collared shirt. A gold engraved crest ring from Dartmouth glinted off his right ring finger.

"Come on," he said. "I need to give you your Christmas present."

"Martin."

His blue eyes were clear, determined, and I thought maybe I underestimated how much he'd actually drank. The Real Estate Temptress glanced in our direction. Her hair was dark and wavy, her eyes dark too, a softer copy of me without the more prominent, practically 3-D features of a Greek. I didn't have to worry. By her glance that turned into a glare, she'd be barging in on us real soon.

"It's not anything I bought in a store. I'm just asking you to go out on the balcony with me and hear me out."

The party was held on the second floor in a conference room of a trendy hotel in West Hollywood that had once been an apartment building. Only judges and lawyers and their significant others were in attendance. I was one of the rare few who also invited my assistant. Part of me knew better than to follow Martin out onto the balcony.

My mind worked the angles. Given it was a shallow drop, he couldn't push me off in a rage without me doing more than spraining an ankle. The other part of me was curious what he wanted to give me that required no money but would most definitely have strings attached. I assumed it was a well paying job at a litigious-happy law firm in Bel Air or Beverly Hills—divorces and DUIs of the rich and wealthier. Martin was often seen winning rounds of golf against high priced defense lawyers. I would turn the offer down, of course, but thank him in order to maintain our increasing span of civility.

High in the distance I thought I could make out the glowing white H of the Hollywood sign against the purple hulk of the hills. I was sharing this view with the wrong man all because I'd gone to the bar for another drink alone, without Grant, when I should've suggested we leave the party early.

"Okay, Martin," I said. "You have me out here. What is it?"

"I've been through your mother's file…"

"She's none of your goddamn business."

"I know she escaped over twenty years ago."

I wasn't expecting him to use his power as a judge to rifle through my mother's case. My life had been stripped bare and then dissected, Martin pulling only the useful parts out.

He leaned against the railing, either relaxed some by being outdoors or by getting all he knew off his chest.

"It's an unbelievable story. Typical the LAPD dropped the ball. With so many fresh murders on their desks every day, there's no time to reconsider the whereabouts of an old woman now in her sixties who, how shall we say, lost her cool one night."

"What the hell are you doing, Martin."

"I want to keep seeing you."

He gestured toward the window that was covered by a sheer drape. Nondescript, blurred bodies were only visible.

"Come on, Ava. You must understand what I'm saying. You saw her. I'm getting married myself to a beautiful girl. But you and I? We have something that goes beyond vows. We'll have this one shared secret."

"What secret?"

Martin took both of my hands in his. His palms were cold from the glass of hard liquor on ice, and I shivered.

"I have resources, Ava. I can make it stop, how she must haunt you every day. All you have to do is agree to a relationship with me, and I will find your mother for you. Alive or dead. And when she's found, I'll do whatever it is you want me to with her."

What he was proposing was frightening primarily because I found myself unable to outright refuse it.

CHAPTER SEVENTEEN

SELF-DEFENSE

Someone has been following me since I left my house in Grant's car. *I have resources, Ava.* That night out on the hotel balcony will not leave my mind. Martin's promise to take control over things in my life went beyond finding my mother. It included finding out everything about me and those I love. It explains the white mini-truck two car lengths behind me since I turned onto Cahuenga Boulevard.

I remember the truck from my street, a flash of the driver's profile, how he'd slowed down as if he was lost. There had been no pieces of wood or other construction materials in the flatbed.

To make sure I'm not jumping to conclusions, I make an abrupt right at the corner of Miceli's, a cozy

Italian restaurant where the servers boast black and white head shots on the wall. From table to table they belt out Broadway showtunes while passing out baskets of garlic bread and bottles of Chianti. Grant and I love eating dinner here on the weekends, lasagna crammed with fresh spinach for me, an entire medium pepperoni pizza for him, and then we drive less than a mile to Universal City Walk and catch a movie, at least part of one.

After three years of marriage we haven't grown tired of pawing each other in the back row like teenagers because the passion between us has not waned. It has become a necessary part of our daily lives which is not the same as calling it routine, and why news of the underage Latina girl had come out of nowhere. Her allegations didn't make any sense whether they were in broken or perfect English.

For the first time since Grant has gone missing real tears form in my eyes, and I swipe at them with the back of my hand.

I don't have time to cry.

At the end of the cul-de-sac, I swing Grant's car around, ready for the oncoming headlights of the man in the mini-truck.

The side street is dark by city standards. Flashes of blue fill the front windows of a couple houses from TV's and computer screens and the street lamps give off a smoggy pink glow. Reflective signs are posted everywhere that parking on the curb is illegal unless you're a resident. I try and picture the side of the man's face in the hopes I can somehow fill out the rest, but all I saw was dark skin, dark hair, not even the color of his eyes. Seconds turn into minutes and a curtain moves in one of the well-lit houses. The cops might be called on me if I stick around idling in the center of the street much longer.

At the corner where Miceli's stands, cars continue rushing past in the brightness of the boulevard yet none come my way. Could the guy in the mini-truck know this area enough to realize I've trapped myself? All he has to do is be patient and wait for me to drive back out onto the boulevard? Or has Martin gotten what he wanted by putting a good scare into me, breaking into my home without having broken any glass? It wouldn't be hard for him to get his hands on my keys.

When I was in trial in a courtroom downstairs I kept my purse in my office, the door usually unlocked because Monica was at her desk. Even though Monica wasn't interested in men, at least not sexually, Martin could charm the pants off her in another way. Monica loved the Lakers and sometimes he'd drop by to talk three point shots and the starting line-up with her, offering her the pair of courtside season seats he rarely used. As a show of thanks, she once fetched his dry cleaning for him. That was just one opportune time he would've had the all clear to take my keys and make a copy of them.

I fumble for my cell phone on the passenger seat and press the number that's programmed for my father's house.

He picks up on the first ring.

"Kitsoli," he says. "It's about time you called me back."

Hearing my father's voice is a relief, the substance of it, how flesh and bone real he sounds compared to other men who claim to love me like Martin then break into my house without a trace or my husband who vanishes in the night from my bed. My father is my center. He is my sanity. He'll know what to do about the mess of the last forty-eight hours. Even lying in a pool of his own blood after having been shot, my father gave me instructions to call his friend Ed from the force instead of calling 911.

"I'm on my way over, Dad," I say before hanging up.

On the Ventura freeway, bumper to bumper with the evening commuters, there is no sign of the man in the mini-truck. With so many witnesses surrounding me, I strangely feel more protected than I have in days.

◆

MORE THAN ONCE I check the rear view mirror as I get off the freeway and coast through two green lights before reaching my father's street. The lights in the family room are on. Martin was right about the guilt I feel every time my father wheels toward me in his chair, but not because I'd stood there and allowed the shooting to happen. It was because I was the one who set my mother off.

A woman had called earlier that day claiming to be a loan officer. She could guarantee a reduction of a hundred dollars each month if my father refinanced the house. My mother listened, her face hardening, unconvinced at figures and forms that would need to be filled out. Iris saw it for what it was—an elaborate lie to cover up an affair.

"How dare that no good *tsoula* call this house."

My mother came here from the islands with her family when she was seven years old. She'd learned English in school and often translated for her parents, but when she was upset and feelings got the better of her, the Greek came out.

"Mom," I had tried to reason with her. "If that woman was cheating with Dad she would've just hung up once you answered."

My mother slapped my face and I felt my cheek nicked from the diamond stone in her wedding ring. Recently she'd lost so much weight that the band practically spun on her finger. Her eyes went wild with a rage that suddenly seemed disconnected from what we'd been fighting about.

I held the side of my cheek, the welt that instantly rose up. Tearing up in front of my mother, this physically stunning monster, was something I would not do.

There was the smell of roasted lamb burning in the oven. My mother was too preoccupied with the phone call to remember our meal. She hadn't even thought to change out of the pink bathrobe she'd worn since this morning tinged brown at the terry cloth lapel with coffee.

Anger bloomed in my chest. This woman had robbed me of regular six o'clock dinners seated at the table with both my parents asking about my day. She had robbed me of the Friday night TV line-up sprawled on the family room floor with a package of Red Vines licorice and a can of soda. She had robbed me of what so many other children take for granted. She had robbed me of *home*.

"I'm not your daughter," I yelled in her face. "I'm Dad's daughter."

My father forgave her for everything, the spontaneous deliveries of expensive appliances or furniture we couldn't afford and had no room for, her made-up dramas that played out in our house as if they were real. Always I'd hear my father make excuses. He'd apologize for the senseless just to calm her down, and I was tired of it. I was tired of her. "You're just a psycho I'm stuck having to babysit. That's why he has to work two jobs. That's why he's never here. If you hate your life with us so much, I wish you'd just kill yourself. You know where Dad keeps his guns."

For a moment the gravity of what I said sunk in. My mother listened, then nodded, the fight draining out of her. In the robe she could've just come out of a long bath.

I wrapped my arms around her tight.

"Mom, I'm sorry. I didn't mean what I said."

My mother returned the squeeze. Her breath was sour from not brushing her teeth and she pulled back to get a better look at me. Her face was unforgettable without even a touch of make-up.

"I could never let another woman take my family," she explained, "I'd kill your father first and then you."

Instinctively, I pushed my mother off and ran for my room where I called my father. The words burst out of me, hardly making sense, but he made me stay on the line until he got home. What seemed like forever was less than ten minutes. An ugly argument erupted between my parents right when he walked through the door. This time my father wasn't backing down.

My mother wasn't so crazy that she didn't think to raise the volume of the TV first so the neighbors wouldn't hear and call for help. After my father shouted he was leaving, things grew deadly quiet. My mother had gone to their bedroom to get the .32 Beretta my father kept in his dresser drawer. She loaded it with the hollow bullets, the kind that expand on impact.

My father came into my room and laid a heavy hand on my back. "Hurry up, Kitsoli. Pack a bag." We were going to Ed's house. He lived a few blocks away.

In the police report it states my father had mistakenly left the loaded weapon out on the coffee table. There was no premeditation, only the heat of the moment when my mother picked up the gun, thinking it was empty, the way my father kept all of his guns. She'd pointed it at him in an attempt to grab his attention. She'd never expected the gun to actually go off.

Years before, after Iris's parents moved back to Greece, my papou died of a heart attack. My yia yia held out for three and a half months before she died too. The doctors couldn't explain it except to say they'd seen it happen before between couples—a form of natural

law that defies medicine—one spouse cannot physically
survive without the other.

◆

I PULL GRANT'S CAR into the driveway of my father's
home. This time I make sure I pick up Grant's cell
phone so I don't keep getting it confused with mine. I
stash my phone in the glove compartment. Grant has
one missed call. I play back the message. It's Reynolds's
female secretary, the one who annihilated me that night
Grant and I had reservations at Westley's. A reminder
call to Grant that her boss would like to speak with him
before their scheduled appearance in court on Monday.
I love how everyone sidesteps the word *incarceration*.
A year in prison could be an intolerable thought to a
man who comes and goes as he pleases, who runs two
and a half miles in a different direction every morning
because he likes to change things up. Suicide creeps into
my head again, the claimed bottle of Seconal. Martin's
little domestic demonstration with the table setting
and flowers might be a coincidence, his twisted show
of support for me—*I'll be there for you when your rapist
husband is locked away.*

My husband's body could be lost to the desert, and
I've left it there to chase leads that aren't panning out.
The Do Not Disturb sign on the door of our hotel room
would only work for so long. Staff would soon need to
see somebody come in or out of the room. They'd need
to see a live body. Each hotel card key, whether it's used

or not, shows a record at the front desk and I have been gone all day. Any minute now hotel security might let themselves in and have a look around. The police would be called and Grant's identity known.

I plan to head back down to the desert but there are two things I need from my father first—a phone call he'll have to place from Grant's cell phone to a certain defense lawyer's office to establish my missing husband's whereabouts.

It won't matter that my father doesn't sound like Grant. Reynolds will play back the message in the morning only half listening anyway, still hung over from the night before. The trial was over, the loss miniscule when taken into consideration that most people thought his client was guilty. The last bill no doubt is in the mail and now it was just about the final court appearance, standing alongside his client at the defense table one more time before Grant is shackled in his suit and escorted out of the room to serve a stint in prison he probably deserved anyway.

The other thing I'll need is an unregistered gun for protection because the white mini-truck is back, parked across the street, two houses down, in the dark space between street lamps. It is no longer a question of rationality or fear. The evidence is in the headlights that have flicked off yet the driver is not getting out.

CHAPTER EIGHTEEN

HELPLESS

To the driver in the mini-truck my father might first seem like an easy mark. He's in his wheelchair beside the steel ramp that now covers the porch steps. His Buick is parked in the driveway with the blue handicapped placard hanging from the rearview mirror. My father is anything but disabled. In high school he was a champion wrestler and now because of his useless legs he's overcompensated so that his upper body, his forearms and biceps are weightlifter strong. All he'd have to do is fall out of the wheelchair. The equal playing field would be the floor where he could put any man in a killer chokehold.

The guy in the parked mini-truck could be anyone, someone Martin hired to keep an eye on me or even one of the Latina Girl's relatives. Retribution for that afternoon in the courtroom hall when my own brand of Spanish chased the Latina Girl's mother into the women's restroom, so upset she left her knitting needles and yarn behind.

My father waves to me as I get out of the car. Typically dressed in a flannel button down shirt and jeans, he also has on running shoes, an old habit of preparedness at all times that didn't die after the shooting. He still thinks like a cop and he needs to be able to react and react quickly. I've never seen my father completely relax in socks and sweatpants because of the possibility that an intruder could barge in. Rarely does he ever take off his glasses either. He gives a quick glance down the street, notices the truck but is more taken by the fact I've driven here in Grant's Audi.

"You came alone?" he asks.

"Grant couldn't make it," I say. I am uncomfortable being outside in full view and I touch my father on the shoulder before beating him back into the house.

Inside he turns down the evening news. The entire house smells of the dinner he probably made from scratch. Retirement turned him into a great cook, a fully functional one who even does his own grocery shopping. No health care worker like Edna comes by to check in on him. For some time now he's mastered the use of that metal arm for the high cabinets in the kitchen, though he learned not to risk it by bringing down any item made of glass. I can't think of when I ate last, possibly the late night half of a hamburger and fries.

A heaping plate of spaghetti with Italian meat sauce, mixed Greek style with too much oregano, is on the coffee table for me, along with a fork and a checkered linen napkin. Though I'm starving, I just pick at a plump breadstick sprinkled in parmesan. A healthy appetite won't look right, not even to my father after he hears what I have to say about Grant. With the drapes closed, seated on the years old couch that is practically new because my father prefers his chair, everything spills out of me—waking up in the hotel room without Grant, the bottle of Seconal and the constant calls from Grant's lawyer. I leave out Martin and the mini-truck because they both sound like they fit in some other story about some other woman. Besides my father has never known the extent of Martin's manipulations on and off the bench. I always thought Martin's need for me would pass in time. The Real Estate Temptress and the cute red head court reporter and every woman who has come in between, none of them have made me a faint memory. Somehow they've only sharpened his focus on me.

I wouldn't call what Martin has been doing for the past couple of years stalking. It's more like strategizing. The slashed tires is the only act typical of a scorned lover and even that is just speculation on my part, a clichéd move he clearly learned from. Martin has become much more inventive and it is because of what he promised he'll do for me once he finds Iris that has always prevented me from telling anyone, not my father or Grant what Judge Durham is capable of.

"How long has he been gone, Kitsoli."

It takes me a second to realize we're talking about Grant.

"A couple days."

My father's expression turns. I've said something he doesn't like the sound of.

"Have you checked your bank accounts?"

The question is obvious, a no brainer and I am humiliated by my answer.

"No, Dad. All I checked was his wallet he left behind." I know what I sound like, not like a lawyer or a cop's daughter. I sound like a stupid wife in love with her husband with every sign pointing to the fact he's obviously left her. My father and Grant have a cordial relationship, bordering over the years on friendship. But I know my father comes from a generation where men didn't so readily start a relationship with another woman while still married. He doesn't trust Grant.

"Kitsoli, it sounds like he might've…"

"Skipped out on me?" I take a sharp breath that aches in my lungs. Just uttering the words, this possible truth, cuts deep and I feel myself lashing out. "You're thinking he's already driven across the border with a fake passport, maybe even wearing a bad disguise, some kind of stick on beard. He's faked it all, right? He wants me to think he's dead so I stop looking. He wants a life without me because he's too much of a weak-kneed son of a bitch who could never handle a year in prison."

My father is not the type to hug me or falsely tell me everything is going to be all right. He didn't do that when my mother was arrested and he isn't about to do it now. Instead he waits out the silence, the opportunity for me to calm down, an effective interrogator's technique. His diligent patience to let suspects talk themselves tired always got him the most confessions in the precinct.

I think of the Latina Girl, her fingernails chewed down to the pinks, how effective those nubs were when she held them up to cover her face. I think of the weeks and weeks of explicit testimony about how Grant held the back of her neck and forced her mouth toward his crotch in the front seat of the car I've been driving around in all day. Then I feel the heat of his breath in my mouth, the condom I made him wear and I remember the lost hours in between, the fact that I slept through it all and never woke up. How didn't I hear him leave?

The tip of my finger is no longer purple. It's black.

Like mother like daughter. It happened here in the family room when my mother said she loved her husband before blowing a hole in his back.

I lean forward like I can somehow get away from the horrible memory.

"Dad, you don't think I…"

"No, Kitsoli. I don't think *you've* done a goddamn thing. You need to stay focused on what you do know."

Margaret.

She could've given Grant enough cash to make his escape. This could explain the phone call. There would be a satisfying revenge in funding her ex-husband's getaway from the new wife he left her for.

"I'll check our accounts tomorrow," I finally say. If Grant is smart enough to leave without a clue, he's not about to withdraw a telling chunk of cash out of our account. We don't have much money in there to begin with. He would've had to have saved for months without me knowing.

I pull the parking stub out of my pocket and hand it to my father.

"I have somewhere else to try."

My father lifts up his glasses, leaving them on his forehead like he can somehow see better without them.

"There's no readable time stamp."

"I know, but Grant keeps his car immaculate. He has it washed practically every week. And it was right there on the floorboard. He must've just recently parked at this place."

"You realize what neighborhood this is in?"

"I don't plan on going over there until tomorrow in the daylight to check it out." I wait before I say, "I might need some extra protection."

My father understands what I mean. At least now he is beginning to see things the same way I am or maybe he's just appeasing me. The reason doesn't matter.

I take Grant's cell phone from my purse and dial Reynolds's office number, stopping short of pressing the call button.

"I need you to call Grant's lawyer and pretend you're him. Just say you're having a good time, trying to figure things out with your wife before you lose her for an entire year. Please, Dad. The guy has so many clients he'll never realize it isn't Grant's voice."

My father shakes his head, places the phone in his lap and spirals the wheels of his chair into another room. I fight myself not to part the curtain and check on the man in the mini-truck. It's better if he thinks I don't know he's watching.

Hanging on the wall near my father's favorite leather recliner is a black and white picture of my father and Iris, before they were married. It was their engagement photo that appeared in newspapers from Southern California to Athens, Greece. My mother's eyes were different back then, shiny and focused on the life she was making with my father, before the life in her head took over. The two of them smiled off in the distance, the deliberate way photographers used to pose couples as if seeing a glimpse of their future.

In Big Sur Grant and I hired a photographer and instructed him to stay back several yards and catch us in candid shots. A colorful picture of Grant and I huddled close right after we'd said our vows is on the mantle at home. I'm smiling, my eyes closed, leaning in to my groom, and it appears like he's kissing my cheek when really he's whispering, "V, V, V," which has always meant more to me coming from him than an I love you.

My father comes back into the room. A .38 revolver is on his lap instead of Grant's phone.

"Let me hold onto Grant's phone for now. There's a record of where it's been from the cell towers. Whether you realize it or not, you've been giving him an alibi. I don't care how much you love him, I'm not going to let that son of a bitch bring you down with him, do you understand?"

Since I chose that curse word instead of using my husband's name, I guess my father thinks it's time he joined in, too. At the very least my father has rendered Grant an idiot for allowing himself, a successful middle-aged while male, to be caught having any kind of social interaction with an underage girl, in a bar no less. Any defense is an indefensible one.

Giving up Grant's cell phone is a compromise I'm going to have to agree on if I am to get the loaded .38. Unlike so many other witnesses to violent crimes, I am not afraid of guns. My father and I used to go to the shooting range all the time while I was growing up, popping holes into hanging paper human targets. The hours we logged at the range were like a son with his dad playing catch or a mother watching her daughter twirl around in pink tights in dance class. Afterward we'd get a burger and fries, a vanilla malt for him and a chocolate one for me from Canter's on Fairfax. Even after Iris used her husband's own gun on him, my father drove us out to the range and watched me fire off a few rounds because he didn't want me to lose the skill or the nerve. She is with us now as she is every time he and I are together.

This gun my father hands me has threads at the end of the barrel. An attachment is missing, a piece that is considered a Class C felony and ten thousand dollars in fines if caught with it.

"Where's the rest of it?" I ask.

"Kitsoli," my father starts, "If you get into that kind of trouble it'd be better if you call Ed."

"Fine," I say. "I'm not planning to use it," I lie.

The truth is I have no idea if I will have to fire it or not. There is a missing husband to consider and the man in the cheap mini-truck who's waiting to get me alone, who may or may not have just invaded my home on Martin's orders.

Before I leave my father returns with what I've asked for. The missing piece is a silencer. They're practically used only as props now in Hollywood films when someone wants to kill without anybody nearby hearing a thing. I don't know whether my father got this off the street or a criminal he arrested years ago. It isn't my place to judge where he recovered this most sinister part of a weapon nor is it his place to judge why I want it from him.

My father and I are more alike than my mother and I ever could be. He knows there's more I'm not telling him. The shooting prematurely aged my father and I'm further deepening the lines at his eyes that reach like scars down his cheeks. I'm giving him more reasons to leave messages on my voice mail. A former public defender who knows how to fire a weapon aside, I am his only child, and he can't help but worry.

"Wait it out here, Kitsoli," he says. "In only a couple more days he has to turn himself in. He either will or he won't. You've done enough, standing by him through that three ring circus of a trial. You don't owe him a thing. You never did."

I rise from the couch. For years after my mother disappeared from the hospital, my father called or drove to every homeless shelter, halfway house and every park he could find from the Los Angeles area to San Diego and even up North toward San Francisco. He keeps a sketch in the junk drawer made from an artist friend at the department of what Iris might look like presently in her late sixties.

"He's my husband, Dad. You of all people should know why I can't stop looking."

◆

IT'S NEARLY ELEVEN BY the time I make it back to the resort in Palm Springs. I realize it's not just Grant's alibi I'm preserving, it's my own. The valet takes my car this time because I let him. Before I enter the hotel I look around to make sure no one has followed me. I lost the mini-truck hours ago in my father's neighborhood. Yet I will not be fooled so easily. I know he will show up again. Inside my room, the message light is blinking. A hospital, the police. It is not an overdose I picture but a body left out in the desert, the flesh pulled off the bone by a pack of coyotes, a body that in less than two days might only be identified through a partial finger or a jagged piece of jaw licked clean with the teeth still attached. Something seems wrong in me hoping for graphic news that will so sickly put my mind at ease.

It's Margaret.

She clears her throat instead of a greeting.

"I realize I should've told you the truth about my conversation with Grant." She hesitates. "I'm pregnant. Two and a half months. At forty-three it's beyond high risk. It's a damn miracle." She forces a laugh. "But Lorenzo and I, we're happy. That's the main thing. Grant and I talked about children, but he said you and he never have. You two love each other too much for someone else to get in the way. I thought how strange that sounded, talking about a child in that way. Anyway, that's what he said the other night. And he wished me well like he was going away for a lot longer than one year."

Grant must've told her where we'd be which isn't that hard to believe. Playing it back twice doesn't change the fact she left the message strictly for me as if she somehow sensed there was no risk in Grant hearing what she was saying about him. It was as if she already knew Grant was gone.

CHAPTER NINETEEN

AVOIDANCE

I should've known when my calls kept being ignored by the prosecutor handling Miguel's case that my client was in real trouble. No response meant no plea deal. A costly court trial didn't make sense when Miguel was a first time offender caught with three ounces of marijuana. Technically two or more ounces was considered drug trafficking. On the books the crime was a solid amount of prison time if California prisons weren't so overcrowded. As it stood, hard core criminals with long rap sheets of grand larceny and sexual assault were being released early just to clear the bunks.

But Miguel was no drug dealer. He was no infamous LA Crip or Blood or an even more violent poser gang banger looking for street credibility. He was a nineteen-year-old high school graduate who worked full-time at Home Depot and still lived at home with his mother and father. Miguel's mistake was he'd been caught smoking weed on the wrong street corner at the wrong time of night by the wrong cop.

I knocked on the office door of Theresa Higgins, the thirty-something prosecutor on the case who purposely looked a decade older than me. Premature gray streaked her light brown chin length cut, the sides held back with drugstore barrettes. It was no secret that she and I didn't like each other. Femininity in the courtroom, the male gaze of some of the judges on the bench and the opposing counsel was a hindrance to her.

As a woman who wore her long curly hair down and dressed up in heels, blouses tucked into my tight skirts, I represented the type of feminist she railed against, the kind that underneath that shirt and bra would reveal clean shaven underarms and handle-worthy breasts.

Theresa was a practical dresser, a transplant from the Midwest, Nebraska, I thought. Her style included sensible flats, women's pant suits and not a stitch of make-up. With high ambitions of becoming District Attorney for the city of Los Angeles, she'd inject testosterone and grow stubble on her chin if it meant she'd reach the highest rank any time sooner.

"I meant to return your calls, Ava," she said. The woman didn't look up from the folder split open across her desk. "My hands are really tied here. Too many cases like his have pled out with no consequences. I need to set a precedent for clients like yours. So I've decided we're going to trial."

Behind her propped in the window sill, as a sole form of depressing decoration, was a sad looking plant, still in the black plastic pot it came in, the leaves crisp, the soil dry.

"*His* name is Miguel Santiago. Have you seen the kid's file? It's three ounces, Theresa, not three pounds. He has no priors."

She still wouldn't face me. Her part was in full view, a crooked line of scalp. Something about the way she wouldn't look up at me told me there was more to it than her being self-righteous in the persecution of a teenage pot smoker.

"Which judge will be presiding. Don't insult me by telling me you aren't sure yet."

Maybe it was the pressure of the situation that kept her head down or maybe it was the pure shame of it all that she was allowing herself to be played. Certain people in this courthouse carried more clout and even for a Nebraska native, her nyloned feet sweating it out in a pair of Payless fake leather flats, a small favor done now would mean a large payback she could demand later like an assistant DA appointment.

I'd rigged it for nearly twenty-four months not to step one foot in that man's courtroom.

Theresa finally stared straight at me, the case against Miguel already won in her eyes because of the name that came out of her mouth.

"Martin Durham."

◆

MARTIN AND I MET out in the parking lot, a dark place where I knew he felt the most passion for me. It was my choice. I'd waited in my car for him to come out after court was over. For once I was going to be on the offensive. Here in the courthouse parking lot he'd bent down out of sight and knifed my tires and it was in another parking lot that he'd eased my seat back and ripped off my underwear. Violence and sex. So popular in American films yet I was never one who saw the connection between the two until right then.

Surprise registered in his blue eyes when he noticed me heading toward his car. He'd recently exchanged the Volvo with a Lexus sedan, the color still white. Without the wealth and the honorable title, Martin would be a common middle-aged man in Southern California, good looking in his own right with his blond hair that swept intentionally across the front of his forehead giving off the vibe he was an easygoing man without a care in the world. A sailboat in a nearby harbor and a Golden Retriever waiting at the front door of his beach home for his return. He'd have to settle for getting laid by broken women of a certain age range still emotionally bruised from their first marriage, searching in bars and online dating sites for the man who'd heal their hearts.

"Theresa told me you were hearing Miguel Santiago's case," I said. "Isn't three ounces of weed a little beneath you?"

Martin chuckled.

"I'll slum it if it means seeing you in my courtroom again." He leaned back against his car, his arms loosely folded at his chest. "You're nearing your what, second anniversary, with Margaret's husband, right?"

I'd heard from Monica Martin and the Real Estate Temptress were in the process of a divorce. The dig about Grant and me was to be expected.

"I'm sorry about your break-up."

"Don't be." Martin let out a sigh and looked up at the flickering underbelly of a plane that was making its descent into LAX. "I can't seem to find the right woman. Why do you think that is?"

"Maybe you should meet the next one in person first instead of on a billboard."

Martin laughed, deeply this time.

"That's good, Ava. That's good. That mind of yours…"

"I have no room to talk, as we both know."

"No, you sure as hell don't."

"Why do you really want to hear Miguel's case?"

"Now there's your first mistake, Ava." Martin wagged a finger at me.

That gesture alone would be grounds for a divorce if I'd been The Real Estate Temptress.

"You call these lowlifes by their first name," Martin continued. "You care too much. He's a criminal, Ava. God knows how much illegal shit he committed before he finally got caught."

"You haven't answered my question, Martin."

"Your end of the deal."

"We haven't even gone to court over Miguel yet, but since you're bringing it up. It's ridiculous that Theresa won't plead it down to a misdemeanor. Probation or time already served."

"No," Martin said. "Your mother. You never got back to me so I decided to do a little investigating of my own. Do you know where you can find her? Every morning she sits out in a place called Omonia Square in Athens. It's a dangerous place, really, where drug addicts and prostitutes and obviously, crazy people hang out waiting to beg or mug tourists."

Because I'd put Martin off for so long I had assumed he had decided not to look for her.

"How do you know it's her?"

"You want to see a picture." Martin theatrically thudded a hand to his chest. "My word can't be trusted anymore by you? I'm not the one who fucked you over, Ava."

I shook my head, stunned. Her going back to Greece made sense. Why there was no trace of her here in the States. Whitewashed walls and white beaches, her homeland was the dream place where my father envisioned her to be, only not begging with whores and junkies on the dirtiest streets in Athens.

"I broke up with you before I got together with Grant."

"And that makes it all right?"

"I never said that."

"Seems you just did." Martin suddenly came close enough to kiss me and instinctively I took a step back.

"Why didn't you tell me sooner?"

Martin slipped his hand, almost tenderly between my neck and jaw line. Only he could pull off a threat in the guise of a romantic gesture.

"Let me know when you'll hold up your end and I'll show you the picture of Mom."

◆

AT HOME THAT NIGHT I realized what had just happened between Martin and I was the first serious matter I couldn't share with Grant. Maybe it was the second. I'd never told him about the night out on the balcony to begin with. My mother was alive and she was a beggar, in my opinion a harsher punishment than suicide or life in a mental ward.

Grant was stretched out on the couch, still in his work clothes, dress socks on his feet, snacking on handfuls of pistachios without the shells. A financial cable news program was on. Grant loved numbers and didn't see the ticker tape stock market marking the day's rise and falls as taking his work home with him.

He must've seen something wasn't right in the way that I kissed him fast on the lips before I headed to the quiet of our bedroom to change. I said I'd be right back.

It didn't take long for him to fill the doorway of our dimly lit walk-in closet. He was still chewing a pistachio. My blouse was off and he took a quick glance of appreciation at my black lace bra. We would have sex here under one low watt bulb in the walk-in closet. My husband was the only means I knew of to get Martin's touch off me.

"You okay?"

I nodded and unzipped my skirt, hearing it rustle down my bare legs to the floor.

"Just a bad day at work."

"Yeah? How bad?"

"Fuck-your-wife-in-a-closet-bad."

Men are too visual for their own good. It is their weakness and no matter how hard they may want to stay focused, I knew, at least for my husband, the fact I'd stripped down to near nothing made him instantly forget the direct question he asked me much less care to press me about my vague answer.

CHAPTER TWENTY

CONFRONTATION

The full stack of pancakes I've ordered in the hotel's restaurant are worth the overpriced fifteen dollars. Or maybe I'm finally allowing myself to fill my hunger void. Not since the hamburger and fries in the privacy of my own room have I eaten so much. Grant always teases me that I dig into pancakes the way a kid would—drenched in syrup, forking through the center of the soft batter oval, then stopping at the hardened edges.

It is a beautiful morning out here in the desert. Palm trees flickering in the sun, already catching heat, the pool radiating even more light. A shame that I have to leave this dry bright paradise again for a two hour drive to some filthy parking lot on Pico Boulevard in Echo Park.

I have no other choice. The parking stub is my final hand to be played.

Last night I slept some, not enough to feel rested but enough to keep me going without seeing double or nodding off at the wheel. Part of me can't help imagining the unimaginable—handsome Grant appearing through the automatic doors of the hotel. He'd spot me seated at a table in the restaurant and come join me.

"Sorry, V," he'd say. "I didn't mean to put such a scare into you. I don't know. I just had to get away for a little while. Clear my head. Get it ready for prison." He'd shrug, embarrassed at his own feelings. "I couldn't stand for you to see me scared. You've seen me be a selfish prick, lose my temper. *But you've never seen me scared.*"

This scenario like so many others can't explain Grant going anywhere without his wallet, without his own car. Only two days are left before check-out, one final day before Grant has to remand himself for his year long sentence.

I have to believe my husband is coming back.

Martin comes to mind; that he's done something to Grant, though he would have no reason to, not when Grant is about to be physically separated from me with barbed wire and iron bars for the next twelve months— the space between us filled with the cold hard fact Grant is in there for statutory rape. Martin couldn't ask for more. The white roses left inside my house are proof of his celebratory mood. He has no idea Grant is missing.

Business in the hotel restaurant is picking up. Outside the window by the pool a young brunette in a hot pink bikini is setting up camp on a chaise lounge—a color clashing orange and white beach towel courtesy of the hotel, suntan lotion, sunglasses and her smart phone. Her skin is pale which makes her ass look bigger when she lays belly down on the chaise lounge.

If Grant were sitting with me now, would he wait until I wasn't looking and check out that young girl? Would he count on the time it took me to head back into our room to change into my own bathing suit so that he might walk over to the girl, his ultimate goal to chat her right out of those hot pink bikini bottoms? Was she staying with another girlfriend or God forbid, with her parents? Would he get off on this line of questioning the way the prosecutor suggested he got off on the attention of the Latina Girl? Was I getting what was coming to me, marrying a man who proved to me the day I met him that he couldn't stay true to his wife?

At the bottom of my purse, next to my make-up bag and wallet is the loaded .38. I was afraid to leave it in the room in case housekeeping came by. Before I came out for breakfast I stuffed a pair of Grant's socks, boxers and jeans in a plastic dirty laundry bag and scattered his razor, shaving cream and after shave on the bathroom counter.

When the waiter returns with my check I can't help from continuing to keep up appearances and request an order of wheat toast and a cup of hot tea to-go.

"It's for my husband," I explain. I go so far as to reach out and touch the waiter's wrist and watch him blush. "We've only been here a couple days and he's back in our room with the stomach flu."

◆

HEEDING MY FATHER'S ADVICE I stop off at a local bank in Palm Springs and punch in my joint account number at the ATM machine. My father was only half right. The money doesn't add up, not because money has been taken out but because more money has been put in, five thousand dollars more. Grant is an investment banker. For all I know there could be 401K's or other investments he's hidden away for a rainy day, for an entire storm front like the one we've been weathering for the past several months. Now he's cashing out. Five thousand would cover one month's worth of bills and not much else.

My father would tell me it's now over. Don't bother following the last lead. *This insulting amount is the final lead.* Be practical. Start making preparations. The house in Studio City will be taken from me once Grant's bail is revoked and I will have to move back in with my father until I can get back on my feet. But I am not my father. I will not mourn Grant if it turns out he's left me the way my father has spent his life grieving for my mother.

I won't chase a ghost.

There was a reason why my husband parked in that garage in a bad part of LA. I get back inside Grant's Audi.

What I'm following isn't so much a lead as it is the final loose end.

◆

THE PARKING STRUCTURE IS three levels, a couple blocks past the Rampart division of the LAPD and several miles before Pico Boulevard turns into a better area where artsy people with money have pushed out the poor. Parking is six dollars an hour, a flat rate of twelve for the entire day. In the rear view mirror there is no sign of a white mini-truck, but I've checked and rechecked for the entire ride here. Although I'd rather be convinced I'm crazy, I know I was being followed last night. It's almost as if the driver caught a glimpse of what my father handed me and knows it might be wise to back off. Either that or he's gotten better at hanging behind me out of sight.

I pull up to the machine and take out a ticket. The wooden arm bounces upward and I drive up the first concrete ramp of the first level of parking where I find a space, park and get out. The entire place smells like urine. Homeless people probably find a way in at night, hole up and sleep here. I expect to spot one now still camped in between the Toyota hatchbacks and Honda Civics, too drunk or out of his mind to get up yet.

The spaces are unmarked. There are no professional titles where people park daily like the lot where I caught up with Grant's doctor out in Palm Desert. This is not that kind of structure.

My hand is on my gun inside my purse. The trick, as my father has gone over time and time with me before, is not to pull my arm out with the weapon, but blow a hole right through the leather of my purse. In this neighborhood, as a white female in a colorful skirt and sandals, I wouldn't blame a would-be mugger for taking a crack at me. I look like an easy mark.

Outside the structure the sky is white with overcast, June gloom a couple weeks into January. A gas station sits at the corner and Tito's Check Cashing is across the street. The place looks as locked up as a safe deposit box with bars across the windows and screen door.

Grant would have no reason to come here unless it was to wire money somewhere without being noticed.

I cross the street and open the heavy door to Tito's. The place is strangely dead at noon, the hour when people have the most time to send or pick up money while on their lunch break. A fan clicks around air from on top of a glass table marked with permanent cloudy water rings and there is an accompanying turquoise colored couch, the cushions beaten down and stained with grease, yard sale furniture.

An overweight man with gray hair, a wild pair of eye brows and an even bushier white mustache stands behind bullet proof glass, apparently Tito himself. As I get closer, flecks of barbecue chips are stuck in the hair of his mustache, some stringy lettuce too, from an unwrapped sub sandwich that is visible on the desk behind him. The catchall for food above his lip leads me to think there is little chance this man is married.

Tito doesn't bother to greet me. It's as if he already senses I'm no customer. He'd be surprised if he knew the woman standing before him was packing a .38 or maybe he's at a point in his life where nothing surprises him anymore. Even with a police precinct down the street this store must get hit at least once a month. No doubt Tito is packing his own heat on the other side of the glass.

I smile or at least I feel like I've tried to. Matching the right emotion with the right words is a difficult task for me lately. For weeks I sat in the first row of the trial showing to the jury who could've cared less just how supportive I was of my husband. And for these past couple of days I've worn myself out by pretending Grant is somehow coming back to me, that he hasn't ditched me for a new life in some breathtaking and impoverished country where he could live large on very little.

"Good afternoon," I say to the man I think is Tito.

I pull out my wallet and produce Grant's California driver's license, thumbing out his name and our address.

"I was wondering if he's come in here recently?"

The man's face is expressionless, his entire lunch on display in his mustache is equally distracting.

"Que?"

I can't tell whether he only speaks Spanish or if he's using the language to try and get rid of me. But I'm not going anywhere. He will give me the information I'm looking for and I will find my husband.

"Has visto este hombre?"

What I say gets the man to actually take a glance at Grant's tiny picture before he shakes his head. He looks sorry for me like he suspects this is about life and death, and I wish bulletproof glass wasn't separating us. For some reason I could see myself collapsing on that disgusting couch and telling this stranger everything.

"No, seniorita. Nunca lo he visto."

Tito tilts his head as if to cue me it's time to leave his store or indicate I need to try the next building, a rundown apartment complex painted dark brown, the color of raw sewage.

So I do. I head next door, under the cover of the foyer where the mailboxes line up.

None of the last names on the mailboxes look familiar—Bautista, Wilson, Dominguez. I search and search. The names are printed like tiny labels, some curling up at the edges, and I wonder how accurate they really are.

A twenty-something mother with dirty blond hair still wet from the shower pushes a stroller right in front of me, blocking my view of the mailboxes, and I take a step back. The toddler along for the ride looks big enough to walk on his own. The boy's mother doesn't realize her rudeness. Neither does she notice that her boy's tennis shoes are nearly scraping the concrete.

She is too busy laughing to someone on her cell phone.

"Oh my God. I had to fake it or the dumbass would've *kept trying*."

I return to the mailboxes.

Who had Grant been looking for? The Latina Girl lives with her parents in South LA, miles and miles away from here. One of the last names registers. Marquez. Diego Marquez, the "friend" of the Latina Girl who works in the kitchen at Monty's. Marquez is a common name so I open the box up and pull out the mail. A bill from the electric company for Diego Marquez.

I look at my watch. It's nearly one, and Diego, if he is home, will be heading to work soon. It makes no sense why Grant bothered to come here.

The trial was over. He is going to prison whether Diego or even the Latina Girl recant their testimony.

Diego's apartment is on the third floor, 3-F.

Over the railing as I head up the stairs, I notice a shallow pool in the shape of a teardrop. The concrete edges are cracked in spots, dangerous for any kid like the overgrown boy in the stroller I just passed trying to jump in barefoot. It is hard not to assume that in a place like this there is probably little parental supervision.

Three-F appears before I've come up with any kind of a plan to get Diego to talk. I knock on the door with my left hand. Thankfully, the door is without a peephole. My right hand has found its way inside my purse, down to the gun.

There is a girl's high-strung voice and then a guy shouts her down. A few more seconds pass before the door opens up. It's Leena, the Latina Girl's best friend. During the trial she'd sometimes sit in the second row, technically supporting her friend, but most of the time looking down, texting on her phone.

She's in a tight black T-shirt and a pair of boxers, possibly Diego's. Her hair is shoulder-length and a little frizzy like she's just woken up. A silver stud is in her nose that I didn't spot in court when she testified.

Leena looks me up and down, jealousy changing her face.

It angers me how easily she's forgotten about me, my husband, the trial. In her eyes I'm seen as more of a romantic rival than the wife of her best friend's rapist.

"Yeah?" she says like we're in the middle of a conversation. "What do you want?"

I decide it's best not to answer and instead I take our conversation inside the apartment, bumping her shoulder with mine. Leena always struck me as the kind of person who acts tough but doesn't actually push back.

What I notice first besides the stench of cigarette smoke is the thick film of white powder, far thicker than dust, on the coffee table. A glossy magazine is left open, a square cut missing from the page. Somebody had been cutting out portions to fold up bindles of coke, the pages slick so the drug wouldn't stick to the paper. The scissors, scale and the rest of the dope he's been measuring out must be in the back bedroom.

Diego Marquez, one of the prosecution's prime witnesses against my husband, is a drug dealer.

A crucial aspect of Diego's life had been missed by Reynold's investigators. Beyond a blunder, Diego being a drug dealer could've changed the entire outcome of the trial; it could've sullied the innocence of the Latina Girl.

For all anyone knows, she could be one of his couriers. This would explain why she was always meeting up with Diego to supposedly have him walk her home when they live on separate sides of the city. If Grant figured this out too, it doesn't make sense why he didn't say something to me.

It occurs to me I've stepped into something that might not be so easy to get out of.

"I want to know where your friend is," I say to Leena. "Graciela Lopez."

Leena has taken a seat at a table littered with dirty dishes, empty Tecate beer bottles and cigarette butts smashed into the wood.

Why bother with an ashtray.

I'm hoping I can put the pressure on Leena before Diego comes out of the bedroom.

She looks at me again, harder this time, real worry in her eyes. Finally she's made the connection between Grant and me.

"Raci doesn't want no more trouble. I told him that."

"You told who," I say. "You told my husband?"

Out of the corner of my vision I see a blurry figure appear from the bedroom.

Diego.

Something glints in his hand, a switchblade he's been using to cut the dope that he now plans on cutting me with.

"No le digas nada," he orders at Leena.

Leena isn't attractive, not like her friend and I imagine Diego gets her to do just about anything he wants. She shows the nervous obedience of a woman who gets slapped around a lot.

He has on a white muscle shirt, revealing scrawny arms that are all tatted up. Gone is the rubber band, the respectable button down shirt and dress pants from court. He cleaned up nicely, I will give him that. If I wasn't standing in his apartment, I don't think I'd be able to recognize him. His black hair is longer than it appeared in court, down to the middle of his back. Some of the strands thin out over his shoulders, in need of a trim.

Diego laughs. Both of his front teeth are ragged, one practically a stump. I've seen teeth like this before, a case when a guy had his face slammed against a curb. He's looking over at Leena but he's pointing at me, the white woman stupid enough to show up in his apartment asking about things that don't concern a drug dealer.

"Qui en carajos se cree esta hija de puta?"

Leena spats something back, but I'm no longer listening because I'm thinking more about my hand that has been inside my purse this entire time. There is no reason to call Ed like my father suggested because there won't be that kind of mess, at least I'm not planning on it. All I want are answers.

I pull out the .38.

It isn't the weapon that grabs Diego's attention nor is it the fact I've clicked off the safety and I'm pointing the barrel square at his chest. It's the silencer at the end, now that part has shut them both up.

Clearly Diego is not used to a woman getting one up on him, not when he has Leena battered and belittled in her place. Shooting him would be the best thing I could do for Leena who will never probably leave him no matter how many times he puts her down, no matter how many times he strikes her.

Over the years I made too many deals with prosecutors, sparing guys like Diego from doing any time in jail, ordering them into anger management classes they don't attend, restraining orders that are broken before they're even filed with the court.

"Vete a la verga," I say. "Where's my husband?"

"How the fuck should I know?"

Diego shows me his front teeth, a grotesque smile like you might see in a freakshow.

"The motherfucker did this to my teeth and then he left."

"When?"

Diego shrugs.

"Fuck, man, I don't remember. The other day."

All is quiet except for the sound of Leena scribbling something down for me on a slip of paper.

CHAPTER TWENTY-ONE

FLIGHT RISK

Cabo San Lucas. A seashore tourist town in Mexico is not what I'm expecting to see written down in pencil on the scrap of paper Leena hands me on my way out of the apartment. It would've been much more convenient if the Latina Girl was somewhere like Ensinada, a place on the edge of Mexico where I could take my chances and drive there myself. No. I would have to book a red eye flight to get to her.

The Latina Girl is staying at a resort down at the southern-most tip of the country. The drive alone might explain Grant's absence if he took a car—at least eight hours, maybe ten one way. He is risking it because he'd have to cross the border with some form of ID. His passport had been relinquished to the court and part of his bond included, obviously, not leaving the state much less the country. Not so far from here is McArthur Park and it wouldn't be hard for Grant to ask around and be set up within an hour with a new identity, for as low as a c-note.

I head back home to retrieve my own passport. Mrs. Wilkes's tan Oldsmobile is parked out front in her driveway, however there is no sign of the old woman in the yard huddled over her flowers. Inside my home, the first thing I do is take the white roses Martin had placed in my dining room and stuff them down the garbage disposal. The water in the vase gets dumped out, the vase dried with a dish towel and replaced in the cabinet. I don't want any sign of him in my house. The place settings get cleared, too. Martin will not intimidate me into a relationship with him. On Sunday when I return from Palm Springs I will have the locks changed.

Maybe it is the .38 I brandished at Diego or the fact that there is proof now that my husband is alive that has emboldened my every joint. Things might finally be getting under control. The bruise on my arm has practically faded away, my fingernail while still darkened shows the yellowing signs of healing around the edges. I will have to get rid of the gun soon. Even though I didn't fire it there is a slight chance Diego or Leena might report me to the police.

My passport is in a drawer on my side of the desk where Grant and I keep our tax returns and other important documents. Greece is the last stamp, nearly two years before, the last place Grant and I had traveled to, our ten day trip where both of us tanned like natives of the country.

At the time I'd had no idea my mother was panhandling in Athens and the truth is I don't know for sure if this wasn't just another of Martin's manipulations. He never produced the proof and when it comes to the reason why she ran, the bullet she embedded deep into the marrow of my father's spine, I have little or no sympathy for her. She deserves whatever misery may have come to her. How long ago that low key trip to the islands seems now when I'm in such a hurry to leave the States again.

With only three days left before Grant has to be remanded into custody, I don't have much time. I pop open my laptop, boot it up, and log on to a cheap travel site. Booking online is more efficient than showing up at LAX empty handed, ticketless in the hopes a carrier will have room for me on a flight to Cabo. The rates for last minute flights are always high. Maxing out my credit card is of little consequence if I'm successful in tracking down my husband.

The best I can find is a red eye that arrives in Mexico a little after 7:00 a.m., breakfast time. I make sure to book a return flight for later that afternoon, giving me a window of less than nine hours.

No matter how warm and light the beaches may appear, Mexico has a much darker side, and I don't want to be stuck without a timed way out. The crossfire of narco drug wars, their trademark decapitations, the policia shakedowns, these violent stories play out in the news constantly. I hear them from my Mexican students who make the mistake of returning to their roots, their homeland, none of them realizing that US citizenship means they are targeted Americans. One woman, a mother of two, had been ripped out of a commercial bus and imprisoned for three days, five pounds of marijuana found in her duffle bag. She claimed it wasn't hers, that it had been planted by someone else, possibly one of the officers who was questioning her. The bag had been stored out of her sight in a compartment along the side of the bus. It wasn't until her husband came up with the money, "her bail" that ensured her release.

Grant has more than just hours on me, he has days, a white hot trail of rage starting with Diego. The wreckage made of his mouth is punishment for talking, for his testimony against Grant. What might Grant do to the Latina Girl who claimed he raped her? Grant had never laid a rough hand on me, but he'd never been pushed to the limits before either, his reputation ruined, for the rest of his life his name popping up on sites as a predator of teenage girls.

I remember Margaret's warning to me in her gallery that I needed to be careful. She hadn't specified who to watch out for. Herself. Martin or Grant. This same thought came to mind on the night I received the shocking call about Grant's arrest for sexual assault.

You don't know your own husband.

◆

AFTER I RUN A few errands I decide it'll be safest if I wait out the time before my flight seated in an uncomfortable chair in a brightly lit terminal at LAX. I don't want to see my father because he will try and talk me out of the trip. Staying at home for much longer is not an option, not when Martin has proven he has a clean way in whenever he feels like it. The flowers and dinnerware means he has plans for us to share an intimate meal. *He* just hasn't decided *when*.

Before the bank closes I withdraw a thousand dollars, a decent chunk of the money Grant deposited in our account. The bills are thick and I spread them out, a few C-notes in the side pocket of my purse, a couple bills folded under the wire of my bra like a paranoid old lady or a stripper with her tips, and the rest I put in the obvious place, my wallet. The trip to Mexico is only part of why I'm suddenly feeling so vulnerable.

The gun is already wiped down wrapped inside a dish towel on the passenger seat. Our home is not far from the Los Angeles River, a concrete channel that is usually bone dry except for now, after a storm, when the water rushes shallow and fast. I park my car on a dirt road used by maintenance crews alongside a stretch of chain link fence.

I open my car door, grab the gun in the towel, and turn just to be sure there is no one watching me, no driver of a white mini-truck catching this all on tape, a better, more personal means of blackmail for Martin if the man turns out to be on Martin's payroll. Moonlight shines on the tire treads behind me. They are my own and while I catch the occasional car pass on the street a few hundred yards from where I'm standing, no driver will be able to actually see more than a flash of silver from the bumper of the Audi. Definitely too far away to see the make of the car or read the license plate.

The cool night air, coupled with the water nearby is enough to make me sorry I didn't think to change out of my skirt and thin cardigan cover-up before I left the house. I hadn't packed an overnight bag because the one I typically use is resting on a rack in the bungalow down in Palm Springs. Hopefully the fact I was seen earlier at breakfast and the Do Not Disturb card I've slid back in the door will keep away the curious. Given it's the busy weekend the staff may be grateful for one less room to clean, one less impatient call for room service.

The dish towel is heavy with the weight of the gun and the edges flap in the breeze. I stand close to the fence, crouch and put my entire weight into the toss. As a kid with baseball and glove, my father taught me how to throw. The roar of the current is loud and powerful. If a person were caught up in the force, bobbing on the surface, screaming for help, no one could hear it.

The splash of a gun means nothing.

◆

THE FLIGHT IS A little over two hours and I sleep for only one of them, my face smashed up against the window. I could've used that second hour. Thoughts of Grant barging in on the Latina Girl in some small room that gets rented by the week with only a single bed and a kitchenette. He's yelling so hard he's spitting in her face, how she's about to pay for destroying his life. Maybe he shoves her to the floor and her head grazes the corner of the bed, the sharp metal part that holds the mattress in place. The Mexican police are called and Grant gets locked up for attempted murder charges or worse, if the girl doesn't regain consciousness, he'll be locked away for life in a third world jail.

Make no mistake, a Mexican jail is third world compared to a California prison with its government regulated cleanliness, its bunks made with bleached bed sheets and three square meals a day served cafeteria style on plastic trays.

As the plane descends I see the rocky shore of the peninsula, the five star resort hotels placed on the coast like pottery colored Monopoly game pieces. The blue water is cluttered with fishing boats, sailboats and tourists cutting through the waves on jet skis. Grant had talked about almost coming here with Margaret on their honeymoon, but she hadn't felt it was far enough away for her friends to be impressed.

After landing, as we disembark off the plane, I pass my fellow passengers, real tourists, hefty suitcases rolling at their heels. Some of them are slowing down, trying to find baggage claim in an airport that is the size of one terminal at LAX. As entitled Americans maybe they are confused by the signs that are in Spanish first and then English.

My plan is to find a taxi at the curb and take it to the resort Leena wrote down. Without asking, she also gave me her friend's work schedule at the resort.

"Raci don't want no more trouble," she'd said.

That didn't make much sense considering as the victim the Latina Girl received justice, prison time for the man who allegedly raped her.

Cabo boasts three hundred and sixty days of sunshine and today is no different. I'm too early for the Latina Girl's shift to start so I kill some time at a café' across the street from the airport. The all night flight has left me wired and yet I indulge in a strong cup of coffee because I need to be focused when I speak to her. I order two sopapillas, gutting the sides with a fork. Grant gives me a hard time for my sweet tooth in times of stress. "Guess what, V," he'd warn, "your problem will still be there even after that sugar rush."

A plastic bottle of honey is left on the table and I squeeze it, filling the bellies of the light pastry, a sticky breakfast that still doesn't quite satisfy my hunger. I'm not even sure if it's hunger that's eating away at me. It's a need to make things right. It's a need to find my husband.

When I'm through with my meal I choose the first taxi parked at the curb just outside the doors to the airport. The driver, a tall man with a skinny mustache, pops the trunk, then sizes me up, my lack of luggage, then closes the trunk again.

"Hello, Seniorita," he says, and I instantly like his ability to come off as friendly simply by combining our languages.

◆

BONITO ROSAS VILLAS IS right on the El Medano beach, a five star spread with wrought iron gates and plenty of ivy crawling up the terra cotta walls that enclose it for privacy. A valet in a flowery button down shirt opens the car door for me.

I pay the cabbie with American money, twenty dollars more than the cab fare.

"Will you come back in a couple hours?"

He looks confused, but nods. After all, I arrived without luggage to begin with. He holds up two fingers.

"Dos."

Inside the lobby I take a look around, stopping at a booth that is set up for guests interested in signing up for deep sea scuba diving or catching a shuttle to a nearby golf course. There is no sign of the Latina Girl. This is where Leena's information ends. She didn't say for sure what part of the resort her friend works at.

Through the bay windows a free flowing rock waterfall gushes into a pool, splitting the shallow end from the deeper part. A small cave-like bar built in with the pool that includes an underwater bench is set up on the shallow side which leads me to think this is no kid friendly place. It is now close to ten. In less than forty-eight hours my husband will have to turn himself over to the courts. I'm frustrated that I might be wasting precious time by coming all the way down here.

I slip inside an elevator that is just about to close and ride to the second floor of the hotel. Eighties style wicker furniture with palm trees on the cushions greets me as I step off the elevator. I walk the floor, peering in at the rooms with open doors, the rooms with the sound of vacuums coming from them. Every single room I enter I seem to encounter housekeeper after housekeeper, some pushing carts, others making beds, on their knees scrubbing bathroom tubs, all of them surprised to see me but smiling politely at me as they're trained to do. I claim I'm lost and ask in Spanish which way is the elevator. Each encounter is a crushing letdown that weakens me in a way that a night without any real sleep hasn't been able to do.

My search for her goes on for the next forty-five minutes as I check the third floor, the fourth and the final one, the fifth. It isn't until I'm back down on the first floor, in the lobby when I see Graciela. Her long black hair is pulled back in a professional bun except for a couple bobby pins poking out. She hasn't worked here long enough to get the hang of the hairstyle yet. She is not in a housekeeping uniform. Her job is much better than her mother's. She's in a bright Rosas Villas polo shirt tucked into a straight white skirt and unstylish low white satin pumps that you might find on a bride who hates heels.

Walking beside her is a woman probably in her fifties, in the same uniform. The older woman is pointing toward another bar, one on dry land with a thatched roof and bamboo bar stools. The bar is beside the pool but also overlooks the ocean. A clipboard is in the Latina Girl's hands like she is a trainee.

Relief pumps through me like adrenaline. She is in one piece. If Grant had meant any harm he would've inflicted it by now. Her being on the job also means Leena must not have warned her friend I was coming.

I follow the two women through the lobby, outside to the pool and bars. Bowls of tortilla chips and salsa sit out on the countertop the way baskets of popcorn and peanuts are left out in American bars.

The older woman checks her watch, then smiles curtly at the Latina Girl before heading back to the inside of the hotel. Her smile for me is more charming, more practiced because she's mistaken me for a guest.

I suppose in my floral skirt I still have on from the day before I look the part.

The Latina Girl is inspecting the perimeter of the pool, picking up a wet discarded towel on a lounge chair and tossing it in a plastic laundry tub most guests never bother using.

A surprise ambush is what I have in mind, the way she took up space at my husband's table while he was busy looking down at his work, if you are to believe his testimony.

"Excuse me," I say, remembering her line to the jury that gave my husband twelve months in prison. "I'm lost and looking for the restroom."

The Latina Girl whips in my direction, ready to serve, the dutiful employee. Her pleasant smile quickly turns to tightened lips. Unlike her friend, Graciela recognizes me right away. Her eyes appear harsher than they were on the stand lined in black pencil and so much blush is on her cheeks it looks like she's running a fever.

I'm used to seeing her pretty and in tears. "I'm working," she says dumbly.

I point in the direction of the woman she was just speaking with. "You either tell me why you did it or else I'm informing your new boss about your former one, Diego, the coke dealer. He had his ass kicked by the way. I think a five star place like this has a reputation to uphold, don't you?"

The Latina Girl's clipboard clangs to the ground. In one flustered move, she picks it up and gestures toward some tile steps that lead down to the beach. I make her go first.

"Please don't say anything," she says.

Grant was right. Her accent does come and go. She'd spent her entire life in the States, educated in public schools in California. The only accent she may've picked up occurred at home.

"I need this job. I'm starting over."

Not exactly a confession, but it's enough to suggest she was lying all along about Grant forcing himself on her. There was no blow job, no unwrapped condom, no rape. Otherwise she would've called security by now, explained the situation, and had them throw me out. In this case, in this country too, the law is on her side.

The first two buttons of her polo are undone, a perfect fit for the flat of my hand to smash that exposed patch of bare brown skin, and I do it.

I push her hard.

Graciela stumbles back, landing ass first on the sand.

Luckily, the view is too wondrous for the guests who are stretched out on towels and bamboo mats just yards away, their eyes shut from the spectacle. There is all that Cabo sunlight to soak in.

Just the same, I lean over the Latina Girl, keeping my voice low. The last thing I need is security to actually get called on me by someone concerned for Graciela's well-being.

"He never came on to you," I say. "You made the whole thing up. You showed up at his table just like he said."

She struggles to get up, opening her mouth, not to answer me, but to breathe.

The wind has been knocked out of her.

I give her a second to stand, her low heels sinking in the sand, making her height lopsided.

"I'm sorry."

"You're sorry."

Graciela nods.

"I had to lie or else I was going away for five years, maybe six. A cop pulled me and Diego over one night, we were in his car and it got searched. We were arrested for drug possession with intent to sell."

Reynolds' investigators scrutinized her background and she came up clean, no criminal record.

"How'd you get the charges dropped."

"This lady took me to her office and told me I had to do something for a friend of hers. And if I did she promised it would all go away."

I think of Theresa in her knockoff office pantsuits and drugstore barrettes. Not only had she put away Miguel, a kid who only had a couple ounces of marijuana on him, but she's responsible for setting a known drug dealer back out on the streets, selling bindles of coke to customers at Monty's and God knows where else. Ignoring felony drug charges was a big deal. It was more than an oversight, it was a favor.

"Was her name Theresa Higgins? Is she the one who helped get you this job?"

Graciela turns toward the water, the waves that flatten and bubble into sea foam by the time they reach the shore.

"She told me if I lied about your husband I could have a new start. I'm training to be a manager."

My handprint is still impressed on her chest like a heat rash. Part of her bun has come out and dark wisps fly out in every direction. She is frozen in her tracks in the sand, waiting for me to make the next move. Maybe the Latina Girl actually has a conscience or maybe she is just scared that I've cornered her into telling me the truth.

One thing is clear—Grant has not been down here or she would've mentioned him.

For some reason I'm not as angry anymore, I'm stunned. It distresses me too, what I've pushed to the sides for so long. I've known better than to underestimate him.

Martin has used his power as a judge before to put away my client Miguel for the maximum sentence, to use an investigator, no doubt one from the prosecutor's office and find my mother. But he's now gone against his own bench and denied justice. He's altered the lives of Graciela and Diego and turned their crimes against them in order to turn them into his pawns.

I remember Graciela's mother, her reaction, how scared she seemed that day in the courtroom hall. But it hadn't been me that had made her flee that way. She had seen Martin. He'd been standing right behind me when I spoke to her. She, too, knew what he was capable of. All of what he's done has been to ensure Grant is out of the way. All this time Martin had been carefully executing his plan to get back the relationship he had with me before that night I met Grant at the wedding reception. What he's done is no slow burn. It's ice cold. It's nearly inhuman.

In some way I must be responsible. I should've told someone, especially my own husband. Instead I continued to let Martin leave me flowers, stop me in the halls, lead me out to a balcony alone during a party with my husband in the other room. Perverse forms of flattery I somehow became addicted to myself.

I know better than to ask Graciela, but I do it anyway.

"Would you consider flying back to LA and telling your story to the police?"

Graciela shakes her head. She tucks a few strands of flyaway hair behind her ear. The shock of my coming here is wearing off. Already the Latina Girl is starting to put herself back together.

"No way."

"You've taken my husband from me."

"I said I'm sorry."

She bites down on a bobby pin, separating it before winding a chunk of her hair around her finger, then securing it back in her bun with the bobby pin. This close up her bun resembles more of a pin cushion than a hairstyle.

"It's not like he isn't coming back."

"He won't be the same after a year inside. Look at how far you've gone just to avoid the possibility of it." The Latina Girl is unconcerned about the innocent man, my man, she's sending to prison. I've done enough questioning of witnesses on the stand to read her.

"What would happen to my parents if I broke my end of the deal? You going to protect them? They're in California illegally."

For someone who hangs out with a drug dealer and gets arrested for it, she is lost to what a man with real power like Judge Durham has done to her.

"Think about it," I say because the conversation is now over. "*You're* the one who's basically been deported."

CHAPTER TWENTY-TWO

DEATH

LAX is a welcoming sight with noisy birds nesting underneath the skylights and terminals and food parks crammed with anxious people. They are oblivious to one another, either running late for their flight or texting away on their smart phones. This claustrophobic chaos is nothing like the airport in Cabo where everyone is trying to get out of doors not stay inside. I walk with no rush like the unfortunates who come off the red eyes or transcontinental flights. The unknowingness has been its own form of suffering, weighing me down. I've carried it with me for so long I'm not sure how to release it.

My husband is not a rapist.

A part of me has always sensed he didn't do it. I can't say he's innocent because Grant is far from an innocent. The trial proved that much. I need a shower, some sleep. I need to go home, but there's still the problem of Grant's and my things still locked behind a Do Not Disturb sign in a hotel room all the way in Palm Springs. Checkout is tomorrow. Maybe my scenario about Grant needing some time to himself before prison is not so unbelievable after all. The Seconal was because he had to do more than sleep. He had to blank out, at least for a few days, long enough time to regain his strength to face his year long sentence. Once the drug wears off and he's clear headed, he will return.

Outside the automatic doors of the terminal, I turn on my cell. Three calls are from my father, none, of course, are from Grant. My father is forever the suspicious cop and won't understand the significance of the Latina Girl's confession. He'll deflate my belief that Grant is returning. What about the money he left for you in the account, he'd say. What about the fact he hasn't bothered to call you, not once for days since he left.

Curbside, cars pull in and out, within inches of each other, risking accident. Taxis await in a long mustard colored line for passengers that don't seem to be coming and buses steamroll past going faster than the security cop blowing his whistle should allow. He is more concerned with a BMW, the trunk open, idling in the red zone. The driver, a rumpled middle-aged Asian man with bifocals in a business shirt buttoned at the wrists, is holding up traffic by holding onto a woman. A suitcase is next to her. She is about his age with gray-less black hair, cut shoulder length, and she's hugging him back, a public show of affection uncommon in their conservative culture. I wonder if they're married and if so, how long. Their unbreakable embrace that withstands the sharp sound of the officer's whistle blaring in their ears quickly becomes one of the most romantic things I've ever seen.

The light blinks red at the crosswalk indicating I have four seconds left to make it to the other side. I was staring at the Asian couple too long. Across the street is the parking structure where I left Grant's Audi. Since I'm traveling light with a passport and purse, I decide to make a break for it and dash across.

Seconds later I hear the awful squish and thud of flesh colliding with metal, of brakes grinding too late to a halt.

I turn, afraid it might somehow be the Asian couple.

But it isn't. A dark-haired man sprawls on the road, his legs pointing in unnatural angles. I take a step closer, close enough to see blood leaking out of his ear. One set of knuckles are bent, his hand touching the ground as if trying to brace himself to get up. He is not going anywhere. I see it in his eyes that are wide open, unblinking, color leaving his face fast. The man is dead, but just as startling is that I recognize who he is.

He is the man whose face I thought his wife wouldn't be able to pick out in a busy store, the man I assumed was security seeing as he was seated in the bar at the hotel in

Palm Springs, the man whose face I now ironically will never forget. He is a man who must drive a white mini-truck. This is the man who has been following me for days. Who the hell is he? Someone hired by Martin to keep tabs on me or is he part of the Latina Girl's family? Not her father because I caught a good long look at him during the trial and he was bald and fat. Maybe her uncle, what was it, her Uncle Antonio?

A crowd has encircled the body, everyone knowing better than to move him. The bus driver, an older black man in a hotel parking attendant's uniform, is muttering and cursing.

Hitting the man is not the driver's fault since the guy must've crossed seconds after me when the light for the bus driver was most definitely green. But the facts won't matter. Whether he blames himself or not, the driver will no longer trust his reflexes at the wheel.

I am the one who feels like I have blood on my hands.

If I hadn't crossed the street at the last minute he wouldn't have followed straight into the pathway of a bus. I don't want to be around for the questions by the cops, for the paramedics to make a show of checking his vitals before pronouncing him dead. I don't want to know for sure who this man is because no matter how I try and rationalize it, he lost his life trying to keep up with me.

◆

HOURS LATER, IN GRANT'S car, I pass the real eye sore of the desert, the Morongo Casino and Hotel. Vegas lights play off the top windows where there is a dance club. Early on in our marriage, Grant and I went there to celebrate New Year's Eve. We had too much to drink and wound up grinding against each other to thumping music we'd never listened to before, him hard, me wet. Instead of going back to the room for actual sex we took the elevator down to the casino floor and played the same video poker machine at the bar, elbow to elbow.

We weren't each other's one night stand. We were longtime lovers. We were married.

In the morning, after sleep and sobering up with coffee and aspirin, Grant came up behind me while I was taking in the view out our hotel room window of the snow tipped San Giorgino Mountains. He lifted my hair and kissed the back of my neck which was far more intimate than if we'd gone straight to the room after getting hot for each other at the club.

Darkness comes early to the desert in winter and by the time I make the turn on to Highway 111 that delivers me to downtown Palm Springs, the sun has just about lost all color behind the mountains. Tourists and residents alike spill out of the white arches of a Mexican restaurant. Across the street is an art deco eatery with a mosaic of multi-colored tiles and outside on the patio are sets of tables and skinny chairs. Grant and I have eaten there before. They serve exotic burgers made of lamb or ostrich and dull tasting tofu.

As I pull into the hotel waiting for valet, I see the sliver of myself in the rear view mirror. My eyes are bloodshot, the mascara having worn off probably as far back as Mexico. I'm reminded of the before picture of a woman on a late night cosmetics infomercial in need of an expensive make-over.

My driver's side door opens and I give up Grant's car keys because there is no need for the quick escape of self-parking. I've run out of places to look, and I'm tired, bone tired as if I don't lie down soon something in me might break. Tonight I will take a long bath and go through the motions of a person trying to relax, though I won't close my eyes. The image of the dead man lying on the ground at LAX, bleeding to himself on the inside, will reappear and plague me if I do.

Inside the hotel a group of loud guys and one girl are playing pool; the table is lined with sequins around the edges, fake jewels at the handles of each pool stick. In a corner a few steps away, a couple makes out on a purple love seat, the blond man's hand is noticeably worked up the even blonder woman's short skirt. The restaurant where I ate pancakes is lit with candles at every table. Grant and I argued here, we parted in the hallway then came together in our room for schizophrenic sex—the emotional detachment of strangers and the familiarity of spouses. The connection between Grant and I will only ever make sense to the two of us.

The small plate of crumbs and the half-empty to-go cup of tea, Grant's alibi of being sick in the room, have been cleared from the floor beside the hotel room door. I pull off the Do Not Disturb sign that has been slotted in the door for over twenty-four hours. The room is picked up but not clean, just as I left it.

I run hot water in the tub, strip out of the clothes I've worn for close to two days, in two different countries. The warm water swallowing my every limb is enough to help me clear my head.

My husband is not a rapist.

Martin is responsible for all of it, the pretty Latin bait, the arrest, the trial and I would confront him if I hadn't deleted every call he's ever made to me from his cell and home. The new redhead in his bed would be with him if I were to show up at the entrance to the gated community in Newport Beach where he lives.

All my presence would prove is that I couldn't let him go, especially now that my husband is going to prison. After seeing such drama, the redhead court reporter would fight harder to keep him than The Real Estate Temptress.

The tub gets drained and refilled twice before I finally step out and sash myself in a stiff hotel robe. I haven't eaten since the sopapillas from the morning but instead of dinner I order pancakes, along with a bottle of Merlot.

The employee on the other end repeats my order as if she doesn't understand.

"Coming right up, Ma'am." The words are polite and insulting at the same time.

My cell goes off, my father again, and if I don't pick up soon I realize he might send Ed after me, so I answer it.

"Kitsoli," he says. "You need to turn on the news."

Have I somehow already been linked to the man who was run over at LAX or is it Grant? I sit back on the edge of the bed, sinking somewhere further than the mattress.

"I only get local desert channels out here, Dad. What is it?"

"Just get the news on."

I reach for the remote and turn on the TV. It takes a few channels until I reach the local news midway through the seven o'clock hour. A lounge lizard of a man with great hair and an orange face ready for high definition is carrying on enthusiastically about a heat wave. "Ninety degrees, ladies and gentlemen," he says and claps his hands together, "right smack in the middle of January."

In the next segment a grainy black and white shot appears of a man in a baseball cap, driving a dark sports car. Underneath the footage is the headline, "Missing Superior Court Judge of Los Angeles."

My father must be able to overhear the sound of my TV because he begins filling in the rest of the story.

"Guess he's been gone for over two days now. Up and drove off one night and hasn't been seen since." My father's voice is revved up, the cop in him memorizing every detail. "No use of his credit cards, no sighting of him, just vanished. His girlfriend was in the house, said she slept through the whole thing."

All I can focus on is the glaring fact that it was a Thursday when Martin drove off which means he'd be in the white Lexus, not the black Porsche. Someone might've encouraged him against his will from the shadows of the backseat.

"I hope they find him."

I force the words out of my mouth because that's what I'm supposed to say at a time like this.

"He's a former colleague. I went out on a few dates with him years ago."

My father gets quiet on the other end, putting things together himself. Two men linked to the same woman who both go missing at the same time is no coincidence.

"That's what I thought, Kitsoli." Then he adds, because he finally knows just as I do what's really happened, "You and Grant, you two have a good last night down there in the desert."

It's not that I don't know my husband, it's that I've misjudged him, what he's capable of doing to protect me, to protect us, our marriage. He must've figured out Martin's plan long before his run-in with Diego. Maybe he started to question things as early as that night I came home so upset after Martin told me about my mother begging on the streets in Greece. Maybe he saw me even before that, walking with Martin out to the balcony at the Christmas party. Then Grant's arrest, his conviction only convinced him to construct his own airtight plan so he wouldn't have to worry about me while serving out his sentence.

After I hung up with my father I checked Grant's belongings again. The one thing I'd missed, the one thing that would've clued me in that he was planning on coming back was his hotel card key. I feel so stupid for not having caught something so obvious, but the car keys, the wallet, his cell phone was too much evidence to prove he'd left without a trace.

What else had been left for me to find? His cell phone with Margaret's number as the last call, the parking stub under the seat. Were they a means of keeping me busy while he was murdering the man I'd been involved with before him? My husband knows I wouldn't go to the cops, but he also must've known I wouldn't just sit around. I'd go looking for him. Leading me to a drug dealer's apartment was dangerous, maybe too dangerous. I might be reaching, but how else could Grant get me to find out the truth about the Latina Girl?

◆

THE HOTEL ROOM IS locked yet I've left off the safety bolt so all he has to do is slide in the hotel card key and let himself in.

And he does.

Sometime in the middle of the night, a little after three, I hear the electric click of the door unlocking. I'm lying on my side, my back to the door. There is the light from the hallway, the give of a man's heavy footsteps on the carpet. For a moment he stands perfectly still, taking in my form on the bed before slowly shutting the door in order not to wake me.

Most wives would push down on that tiny brass button on the nightstand for the lamp that would practically light up the entire room and demand answers. I am not that kind of wife, or maybe it is the lawyer in me.

Answers would make me an accessory to my husband's crimes. It would make me an accessory to murder. Already I am inadvertently responsible for one man's death whoever he may be.

Martin is another.

The tape from the news program plays over in my mind. Grant must've used a gun on Martin to drive himself to his own end in the same sports car where he'd lowered the passenger seat and had gone down on me. I doubt Grant knew about that and I doubt even more that Martin offered it up. Grant must've forced Martin to swallow the entire bottle of Seconal, an overdose or a means of knocking him out to kill him in some other way.

Grant is kicking off his shoes, peeling off his socks, there is the jangle of his pants weighted down with loose change, a leather belt settling on the floor. I imagine his shirt has come off, too. His boxers won't because he doesn't want to come on too strong.

I clutch the sheets, every instinct calling for me to roll over and meet his body with mine. The mattress dips then balances as Grant joins me in bed. His skin smells different, a detergent odor from a heavy duty soap we don't use at home. He's cleaned up somewhere before coming back to me.

I am naked and his hands start warm at my waist, getting to know the geography of me once again, the way he did in bed in my apartment after he left Margaret. I find myself searching too, in the feel of his touch, how Grant did it, how he murdered the man who would do anything except kill to get me back. Martin had underestimated my husband's love for me, his passion unrestricted by any crime or rules of law. It lacks conscience or remorse. It is raw instinct, equal in its intensity to that of my mother's deranged feelings for my father, and for once, I can see why she told my father she loved him before pulling the trigger.

"V," Grant whispers thick and hard in my ear. "V," he says again as if confirming to himself he's really in bed with me.

I take his hand that most likely choked the life out of my former boyfriend, the hand that has calloused up while digging the grave in a patch of desert from here to Arizona or here to Nevada. I can only hope he's covered his tracks because I don't want to lose him, I can't lose him for any longer than I've already prepared to endure starting Monday.

I guide his hand down between my thighs and I part my legs. Grant pulls off his boxers with his free hand. He inches closer and I feel my husband move deep inside me the way he did that afternoon in Nafplio when we stared off at the endless waters, the way he did that night here that seems so long ago when he sensed the shame was too much and I couldn't bear to look at him.

In the morning he can explain what he feels he must, we can talk. All of what will be said, the words we'll use are secondary because my husband and I, we are now, we are always these two lovers first.

CHAPTER TWENTY-THREE

COVER-UP

Four months into Grant's sentence Reynolds shows up unexpectedly at the end of my California Law class, pushing toward me against the tide of students flowing out of the lecture hall. From the pit where I still stand behind the podium, I notice he looks healthier, the tell-tale alcoholic flush on his face has cleared. He's even dropped a few pounds, his belt no longer squeezing him in half. His reputation that took a hit by losing Grant's case is now rebounding thanks to a high-profile trial involving a well-known TV veteran actor accused of murdering his daughter's boyfriend, knifing the guy in the chest while he slept in a La-Z-Boy. No previous 911 calls reporting abuse are on record. Though helpful black and white photos of the daughter's bruised neck suddenly surfaced just weeks before the trial began. Supposedly, Reynolds claims, they were hidden away in a safe deposit box at a bank. Theresa Higgins is the lead prosecutor who fought the hard fight to keep the photos out, but without Martin backing her, she has no judicial pull. For once she can't rig the odds. If she doesn't win a case so top heavy in favor of the prosecution, it will be a career ender, a forever stop-gap to future promotion.

Hope tightens up my throat at the thought Reynolds is here to relay the good news. I will not prematurely voice it. My husband is getting out early.

"Impressive," Reynolds says, approaching me in his jury-distance way, "how much you know about the law. I might have to offer you a job at my firm."

I shake my head at the flattery because it falls flat. Something about his visit doesn't feel right. Why would he come all the way here to the university to inform me time has been shaved off my husband's sentence? The fact is he wouldn't, especially when he's trying a case that's kept him at the top of the nightly news cycle.

"Thanks," I answer, playing along. "But I have my hands full teaching prospective prosecutors that just might rival you one day in court and win."

Reynolds chuckles loudly, the echo it makes is unsettling.

"You have been witness to my best moves. Not that they did a damn for your husband's case. You know, they still haven't found that judge…" Reynolds taps a conspicuous finger against the side of his face, a gesture I've never seen him do before. "Durham, that's it. Martin Durham. Never tried a case before him, pulled some strings once and had one rerouted right before it landed on his bench. Word is he's a real cutthroat son of a bitch. He went missing around the same time Grant was remanded."

I shrug off the connection.

Subtlety is hardly Reynolds's strong suit, too many rounds in the courtroom being the brash defense lawyer with yet another slick trick up his tailored sleeve. Like black and white photos taken long after a murder has been committed or an unseen wire taped to his chest recording our entire conversation. Chalk it up to my own paranoia, but this is not some friendly visit.

And I am not so easily deceived. I, too, am a defense lawyer, the truth a malleable thing it's my job to reshape.

Were the cops in the back of an unmarked van now, listening in from a nearby parking lot?

"I don't keep up on anything or anyone from Superior Court, Reynolds. I haven't worked there in years." I gather my notes and folder of collected student papers in one arm, one steady arm, the signal I'm about ready to leave for I am not rattled by hearing the name of the man my husband has murdered. I understand why Grant killed him.

Failure registers on the shyster's face. It doesn't matter how long he draws this exchange out. Reynolds realizes he will get nothing useful for the police out of me because I am the one in control of this conversation.

◆

CHINO MEN'S PRISON IS a good hour away, a drive that takes me out of Los Angeles County, on at least two different freeways, a routine I follow every Saturday without complaint. Behind the spread of chain fencing and spiral wire stand the open dormitories that disturbingly are less than a stoplight away from a public park with swing sets, jungle gym and a soccer field.

The luxury of shared space with other inmates is not for someone like Grant. Classified as the lowest bottom feeder of criminals, a "chomo," prison slang for a child molester, he endures his time behind bars isolated in a cell no bigger than our bathroom for his own safety. He is allowed one hour a day for fresh air or to take a shower. Instead of utilizing the communal shower he sponge bathes using the tiny steel sink in his cell having seen one too many horror documentaries about the free-for-all that oftentimes occurs between hard spray and tile. "It's the place where guards like to turn their backs," Grant insists.

No one here knows my husband is innocent. On occasion one of the female prison guards responsible for ushering me into the visitation phone banks shoots me a pitiful look that says—*Damn, you're stupid for sticking by him.* And just as I did for the jury during Grant's trial, I glance down, playing a new role, that of a gullible wife in denial that her husband is a convicted statutory rapist.

Through the bulletproof glass, Grant appears in a baggy dark blue jumpsuit, more gray has edged into his hair but he looks no worse for wear. His arms are pale yet still muscled from daily push-ups on the concrete floor of his cell. With or without expensive testosterone shots or daily five mile runs, Grant is not a man who will let himself go.

He grins as he straddles a stool cemented into the floor and picks up the receiver.

"There's my beautiful, V."

His voice sounds scratchy, far away even though it's just a transparent barrier separating us.

I smile back. Sometimes seeing him in person makes me feel lonelier than at night when I pull down the sheet, about to slip into our empty bed for another bout of fitful sleep. My husband's presence is as haunting to me as his absence. Before this, the longest time he and I had been apart were those few days, measurable by hours, when I awoke without him at the resort in Palm Springs then began the search.

"You act as if I don't come here every weekend like clockwork. I don't know, maybe I should miss a week..."

"Don't you dare."

Grant shifts his head slightly to the side like he's about to offer something funny, continuing to flirt, but he stops.

"Hey," he says, leaning forward, reading something in my expression that concerns him. "What's going on?"

I am unsure how to answer. As usual, our conversation is being listened in on and it might strike more attention if I don't tell Grant about Reynolds's coming by my class.

"Your former lawyer paid me a visit."

"Yeah?"

"I'm not sure why."

I look away, remembering the condition Grant was in after he did it, his hands, the rocky calluses and the strong soap. They couldn't possibly have put it together that Grant is responsible for Martin's disappearance. It's just a fishing expedition. No clues frustrates investigators into casting the net wider. I stare back at my husband.

"Maybe he has a crush on me."

Grant places his large hand against the glass, stretching out his fingers, a simulation of closeness, of touching me.

"*I* have a crush on you. And don't you forget it."

I nod. My husband and I have taken to communicating in code since he's been locked up. A hand to the glass really means I am saying too much and I need to let him effortlessly change the subject the way he does when we're at a social gathering and someone is getting too political or too drunk. We just have to ride this cursory inquiry of suspicion out because Grant can't be the only person of interest.

Martin has a complicated list of enemies, from half the incarcerated criminals in Southern California to the many women he crossed, dropping them without tact or compassion. His charm gone, Martin's behavior at the tail end of a relationship is unconscionable. Any of his former lovers will confess to that. Someone somewhere had brought up my name to investigators, either Margaret or the other prominent ex, The Real Estate Temptress. I was right in warning my husband he couldn't trust Margaret on the witness stand speaking on his behalf.

But like the police, both women are harmless. They have nothing. In time Grant's name will be slashed from the loaded list of suspects. I grow more confident with each day that my husband has pulled off the perfect crime.

"He came by here, too."

"What did he want?"

"Among other things, to let me know in person that I'll be released three weeks from now."

"Really?"

Grant lowers his hand so that I visibly see he's serious. The "among other things" must've covered questions about Martin. My husband has proven capable of vanishing a person as well as that person's vehicle without a trace. He'll handle any softball interrogation regarding Martin's disappearance by his own lawyer. He had withstood a harder line of questioning by Reynolds in prepping for the trial.

"Overcrowding and good behavior," Grant goes on, his dark brown eyes alive, Martin, the man he killed, already a fading memory. "You have to love our California prison system."

"I love you," I say. It is probably the most heartfelt and damaging thing I could tell anyone. I know this now. I am, after all, the burning motivation behind my husband's lethal act. I nearly killed for him, too. What would I have done in that dank drug-infested apartment had Diego rushed at me with the knife? Would I have pulled the trigger, blowing a hole straight through the pulsing muscle of his heart?

To the outside world, to that critical female prison guard, I either look like a victim of a violent childhood where I witnessed my mother shoot my father in cold blood or an ultimate saint generous enough to give my cheating husband a second chance. In both scenarios I do not know how to save myself and walk away.

Instead of telling me he loves me back, Grant says, "Nafplio. I owe you another sunlit afternoon watching the water from our hotel room."

"We did more than look out at the sea."

Grant lets out a long breath.

"That's all I think about in here."

"So you're telling me it's your porn?"

"You are my fantasy."

The image of Greece is a little different for me. I think of what Martin told me that night on the hotel balcony, how my mother could be found stumbling around, wrapped in rags, in Omonia Square with all the other beggars and crazy people. If true, I have to help her, she is my mother, that part of me that bore witness to an attempted murder and, as it turns out, not exactly an accessory to murder, but complicit to one *after* the fact.

"We might need to make another stop while we're in Greece."

Grant knows I'm speaking of Iris.

"We'll bring her home."

"I wouldn't go that far. Maybe find her a safe place of her own to stay thousands of miles away, *in her own homeland.*"

Grant nods. He will agree to anything I suggest for we are bound, not just by love but by our grave choices to protect that love. We are woven closer than the DNA of a child we've decided we will never conceive.

My husband may have dirtied his hands, he may even have blood on them, but he *has* served his time, even if in secret it's for another crime, a more heinous one that if found out could give him life in prison. For Grant and I, love is no light matter. What we share overshadows a felony charge, a jury's guilty verdict and Grant wrongly having to register as a sex offender. What my husband and I share goes beyond marital vows on a cliff top at Big Sur, several feet deep down in the desert floor to the real whereabouts of the one person who dared and tried to break us apart.

ACKNOWLEDGMENTS

I am grateful to my publisher Tyson Cornell for his bold vision of books and literature. For their professionalism and commitment, special thanks goes to my editor Alice Elmer, Julia Callahan, Andrew Hungate, Hailie Johnson and the rest of the fantastic Rare Bird staff.

Many thanks to Annica Jin-Hendel, Mary Ann Brown, and Julia Drake for reading the early draft of this book.

Last but not least, to my husband Jim Brown for his support and understanding the erratic hours I keep as a writer.